YOU ARE THE DETECTIVE

YOU ARE THE DETECTIVE

the creeping hand murder

MAUREEN JOHNSON & JAY COOPER

HARVILL

AMERICAN NOVELIST MURDERED

Stabbed in Front of a Room Full of People

NO WITNESSES!

The American novelist Roy Peterson, famed for his book *Henderson's Can*, was murdered last night in Mayfair. Mr. Peterson was stabbed to death during a society gathering. According to all present, however, no one went near Mr. Peterson the entire night. He was sitting in a chair by the fire, off by himself, and appeared to be asleep. It was only with the appearance of the police—who had been alerted to come to the address by an anonymous letter—that it was discovered that Mr. Peterson was dead. The murder weapon was found under his chair. How was a man stabbed in a room full of people, yet no one approached him, and no one saw a thing? The crime seems unnatural and has struck fear in the hearts of Londoners.

Undated publicity photograph of Roy Peterson with one of his many cats

MURDER CASE STUMPS POLICE

POLICE BAFFLED BY IMPOSSIBLE CRIME

Police remain baffled by the seemingly impossible murder that took place at 19 Tootley Row. The American novelist Roy Peterson was stabbed in front of six other people—all who claim to have gone nowhere near the victim, and who swear that no one else did either. Only some sort of otherworldly entity—a hand that crept across the room to wield the knife—could have been responsible. Reports have surfaced of a séance gone wrong and possible demonic practices taking place in the house, which is owned by "artist and sometimes poet" Ambrose Belvoir. "He's a queer one," said local resident Mrs. Henrietta Doome. "Very strange people come and go from that house. He wears green suits! I'm not surprised there's been a murder." Many have started calling it "the Creeping Hand Murder," as it seems that only some kind of disembodied hand could have committed the act.

NO PROGRESS IN CREEPING HAND MURDER

Public Demands Answers in Bizarre Death

There have been no developments in the Roy Peterson murder case. "We are deep in our investigation," said Detective Chief Inspector Harold Jensen of Scotland Yard. "We will stop at nothing to get to the bottom of this matter. And no, there were no ghosts involved. There is no murderous creeping hand on the streets of London. Please stop telephoning us with sightings."

NEW SCOTLAND YARD
LONDON, SW1

Telephone:
Whitehall 1212

6 January 1934

Dear Detective,

    I feel certain you will have read about the Creeping Hand murder case that has been all over the newspapers for the last few weeks. I must confess to you privately that we are stumped. We've had our best people look at it. (Even Spilsbury took an interest!) We have come up with nothing and the pressure is mounting from all directions.

    I was hoping I could convince you to have a look and see what you can make of this baffling situation. Attached you will find a brief on the case, as well as the contents of our files and other relevant materials. I have included my personal notes and observations along with the images.

    I eagerly await your thoughts. You may be the only person who can solve this murder. Obviously, this is a confidential matter, so please take the appropriate cautions.

Yours truly,

Harold Jensen

Detective Chief Inspector
of the Metropolitan Police

Photograph of 19 Tootley Row, taken on 27 November, 11:52 P.M.
The murder took place in the sitting room, which is the room with the drawn curtains.

COPY

New Scotland Yard

29.11.33

To: Detective Chief Inspector Jensen,
Special Branch

Sir,

    As requested, my report on the events of the evening of Monday, 27 November.

    At 10:40 P.M. I was dispatched to the premises of Finsdale Fine Tailoring at 8 Higgins Court where I was met by a Mr. Edward Finsdale, the owner and proprietor. He explained that every evening after supper he returns to his shop to work in the quiet from eight o'clock until ten-thirty. When he went to the door to go home for the evening, he found that an envelope had been pushed through the mail slot. He was certain it was not there when he came in at 8:00 P.M. He handed the note to me. It read: Send police to 19 Tootley Row at once. There has been a murder.

    Naturally, he was skeptical, and believed the letter was some sort of joke. Nevertheless, he called the police. I also assumed the note to be a strange joke, but of course had to make certain. I took it into my possession and proceeded to 19 Tootley Row to determine if anything was amiss.

Tootley Row is near the shop, and I was there within a minute or two. I checked the time when I came to the door. It was 10:55 P.M. I knocked, and after a long moment, I was greeted by a man in a red dressing gown with rather long hair. I asked him his name and if he was the owner of the property. He said that he was, and that his name was Ambrose Belvoir. I apologized for disturbing him, but he said, "Not at all, darling boy! You must be the last of the ghosts. Come in. We're having a most diverting little evening."

I stepped into the entry hall and explained that the police had received information that someone at this address was in distress. "Well," he said, "we are out of ice. Do they send the police around for that?"

I said that ice distribution was not amongst our duties.

"Shame," he said. "What a world it would be if the police went around handing out ice. How marvelous. But come, come. Get warm. Join the haunting."

A strange man, if you don't mind my saying, sir.

I was shown through to a large, dark sitting room—curtains drawn, fire blazing at the far end. The room was decorated in what in some circles they call art, sir, but I could make no sense of it. It all looked like the sort of thing my little girl Millie drew when she had the mumps and the fever took over. I like a nice bit of art, sir, like a good picture of the sea or that painting Whistler did of his mother, but not this sort of rubbish.

There were six people in the room, and unlike Mr. Belvoir, none of them seemed to find the presence of a police officer funny. I will describe how I encountered them, working my way around the room clockwise. In a chair to my left was a very pretty lady with blond hair wearing a black dress and hat. She looked like she might crawl between the chair cushions in fright. There was a woman on the sofa next to her, stout and honest in appearance, and I'd say in service of some kind. Next to her, in a chair by the fire, was a man in a tweed suit, fast asleep. Across from him, on the other side of the fire, a woman who was vaguely familiar, twisting her hands in worry. On the sofa next to her, a fine sort of gentleman. And then, in the chair to right of where I was standing, a rascal of a fellow if I ever saw one. Handsome, but the sort you keep your eye on when there are ladies about.

It struck me that there was something strange about the group. A few looked like they belonged to the bright young set—like Mr. Belvoir, and the blond woman, and the handsome fellow. Yet there was the woman who I learned was a cook, and the older man who I found was a Lord, and the anxious woman by the fire didn't seem as polished as some of the others. And then there was the sleeping man who looked like a university chap. An odd gathering, sir. I thought at first it might have been a seance. My wife, Imogen, has been to three of them and she says all sorts turn up and you sit quiet in dark rooms and talk to ghosts, and Mr. Belvoir had mentioned ghosts and hauntings. I have to admit I was pleased, sir, because I'd quite like to see something like that, but obviously I was on duty and hadn't come to see people talking to ghosts so I stuck to the business at hand.

I explained why I had come, the note mentioning murder, which went down like a lead balloon with all but Mr. Belvoir, who clapped his hands in delight. I asked if anyone in the room had written the note. All replies were in the negative. "Must have been someone in high spirits," Mr. Belvoir said. "Perhaps a friend of mine thought they were being funny." I said there was nothing funny about wasting police time.

I asked if anyone else was in the house. Mr. Ambrose said no, his manservant had the evening off. I asked if I could have a look around and Mr. Belvoir seemed happy enough to oblige. I began in the hall outside the sitting room, which was in a frightful state, with strange objects knocked all about the place. I opened the door to the dining room, which contained even more shocking bits of this art nonsense. (I apologize, sir, but it was monsters eating people and the like, and these were people I thought talked to ghosts—I'm not afraid of ghosts, sir, but I think you need to be respectful of them and I admit it started to worry me being in a place like this.) I also examined the WC.

All of these rooms were empty of people. I also looked upstairs, where I found empty bedrooms and a dressing room. No one was hiding up there.

Mr. Belvoir took me down into the lower level to the kitchen and housekeeping rooms, which again were empty. These, at least, were sensible rooms. However, one pane of the kitchen window—one near the latch—was broken and there was glass in the sink below it. I asked Mr. Belvoir if he was aware that he had a broken window. "I never come down here," he said. "This is George's domain. I didn't entirely know I *had* a kitchen."

Returning upstairs, I was about to leave when I poked my head into the sitting room. The group was talking quietly amongst themselves and stopped as soon as I came to the doorway—all but one. The man by the fire wasn't awake or talking. There was something about him, about the way his position hadn't changed in the slightest, that caught my attention. I asked who he was.

"That's Peterson," Mr. Belvoir said. "He's a famous American novelist. He had a few too many to keep away the cold, I'm afraid. He's been asleep half the night." Mr. Belvoir called to the man, then walked over and shook him by the shoulder. The man in the chair slumped but did not stir. I approached Mr. Peterson and tried to rouse him myself, but when I was closer, I could immediately see that something was amiss. He was not moving at all. I put my hand against his chest to feel for any signs of breathing. There were none. Mr. Peterson was dead. My hand brushed something wet on his left side, and when I withdrew it, saw blood on my fingers.

Some occupants of the room had come over to see what was happening. I said that Mr. Peterson had expired and that they needed to move back. At this, they erupted into shouting and dismay and the room fell into a state of chaos. I more forcefully instructed everyone to return to their seats and not come near the body. I told Mr. Belvoir to telephone the police station. He left the room to use the hall telephone.

I stood back so as not to disturb the body. As I did so, I noticed something under the chair. It was an ice pick, covered in blood. I also noticed, when looking toward the fireplace, the partially burned remains of a letter. It had only just been put in the fire, clearly, so I was able to pull it out with the poker. It was of the poison pen variety, I could see, with cut-out letters.

When Mr. Belvoir returned, I demanded to know the nature of the gathering and find out about what kind of seance this was that ended up with a man being dead. At first, the group quieted and looked at each other nervously, until the woman later identified as Vita Simpson cried out, "We have to tell him!" The older man, identified as Lord Chomley, said, "Quiet, damn you!"

"This is a very good joke, but it's gotten out of hand," said the man identified as Felix Darlington. "We've gotten these letters, you see. Poison pen, you know. Dastardly stuff. And we were told to come here."

He pulled a letter from his pocket and showed it to me. It was a note instructing him to come to 19 Tootley Row. I soon established that everyone in the room had gotten similar notes, each one specifying an arrival time—each ten minutes apart. I tell you, sir, I felt better about this. I can handle letters. Much better than murderous ghosts.

Of course, I asked about everyone's movements. They were all quite adamant that no one had gone anywhere near Mr. Peterson the entire evening. "Then how do you explain the fact that he's sitting here murdered, a wound in his side and the weapon on the floor?" No one could.

I collected all the letters and notes. At this point, other officers arrived, including yourself, sir. I continued my work under your direction.

This concludes my report on the events of that evening.

Your obedient servant,

Reginald Wilkins

Reginald Wilkins, Constable

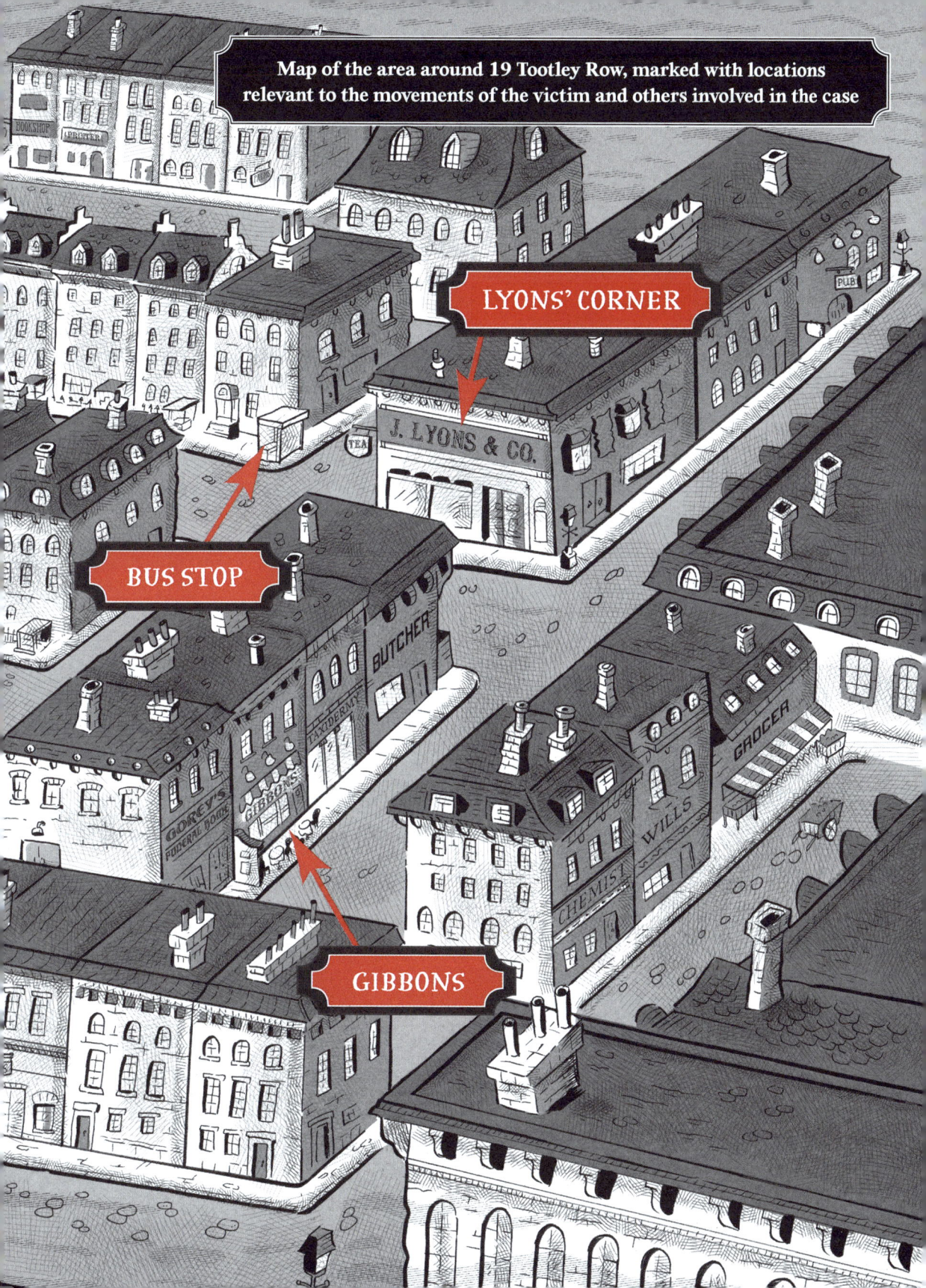

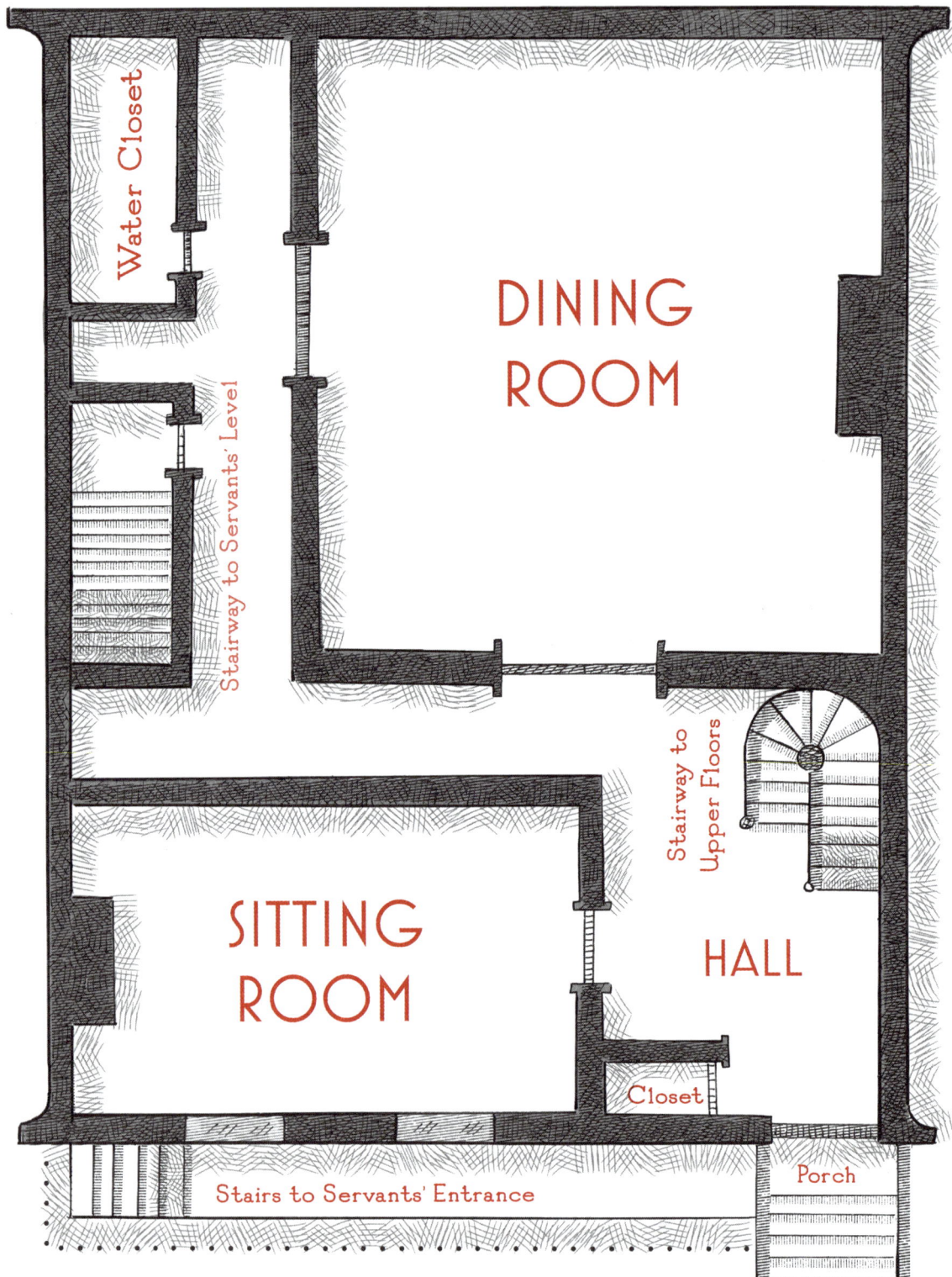

Main floor layout, 19 Tootley Row

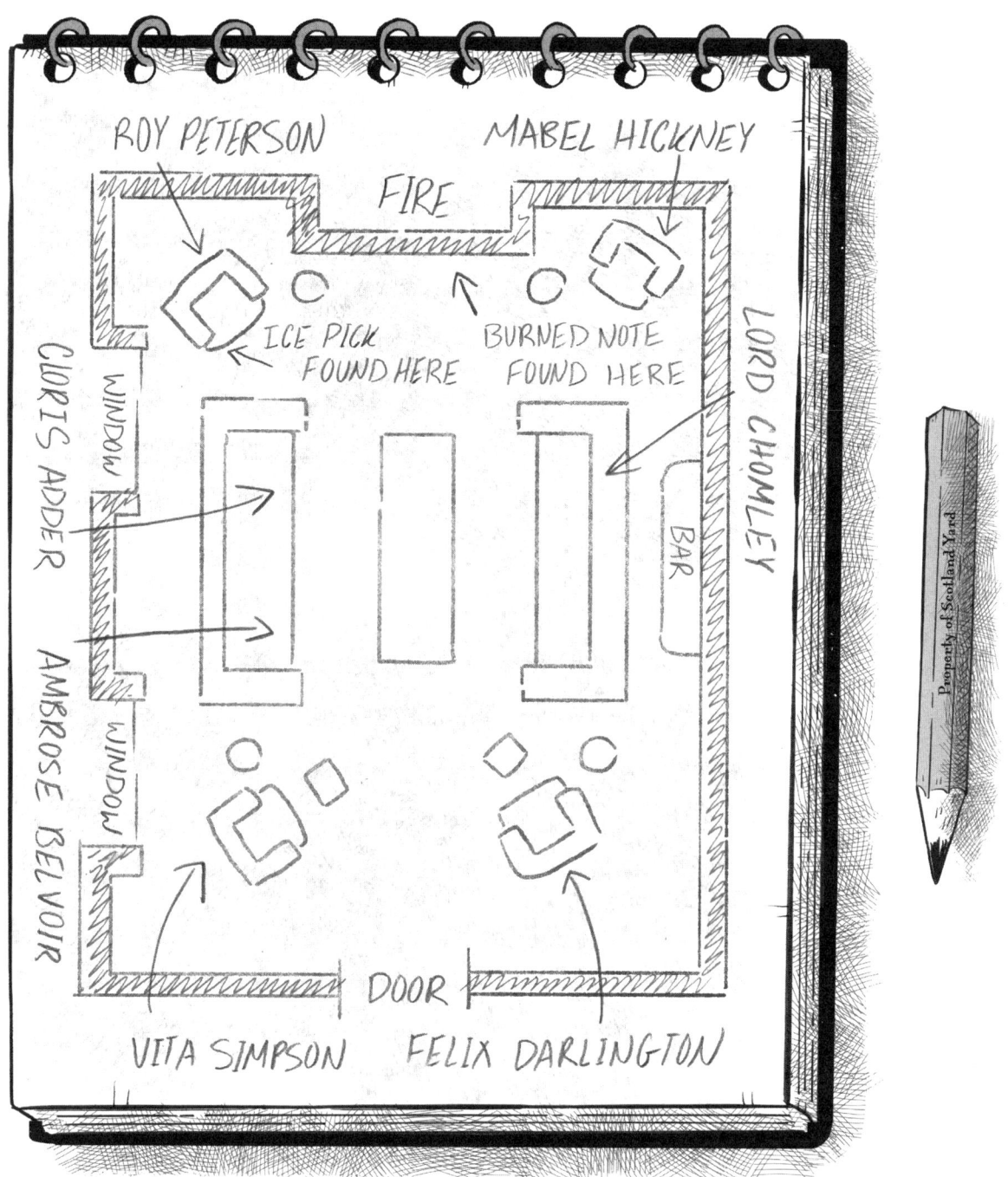

Wilkins's notes on the scene as he encountered it

OBSERVATIONS AND MEDICAL FINDINGS

Roy Peterson was in a chair to the left of the fireplace (from the vantage point of the doorway). Rigor was just starting to set in when I arrived. Due to the dark suit and the deep color of the chair, almost no blood was visible to the naked eye. The medical examination showed that Mr. Peterson was killed with one puncture to the upper left side of his chest, entering between the ribs at a slight downward angle. It was a relatively shallow wound that pierced the spleen. There were no other fresh marks or traces of injury on the body, save for a razor nick near his right ear and a small, light bruise on his left temple.

The cause of death was internal bleeding, which would have occurred within a relatively short period of time, certainly no more than an hour or so, but likely much less. The ice pick under Mr. Peterson's chair was found to be an exact match to the wound.

The examining doctor found morphine in Mr. Peterson's body. The dose was certainly high enough to impair Mr. Peterson's ability to function, but it would not have killed him. There were no traces of tablets in Mr. Peterson's stomach, which still contained the remains of a meal of lamb stew with potatoes. Given this and the fact that no needle puncture marks were found on his body, Mr. Peterson must have consumed the morphine in liquid or a ground, powdered form. No morphine was found on Mr. Peterson's person or in his flat. He had a half-full glass of whisky by his side at the time of his death. This was examined and found to be untainted by any drug.

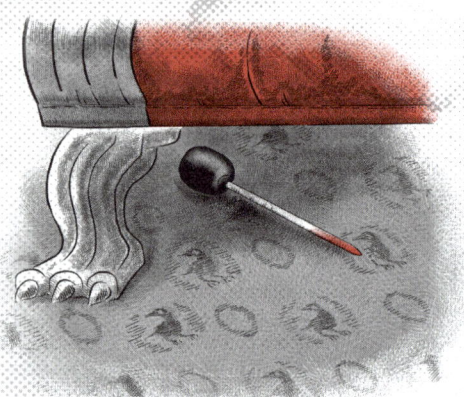

Photograph of ice pick on floor, taken 12:10 A.M.

The ice pick was found under the chair, point facing the room. Our tests proved this to be the murder weapon. There were no fingerprints on it.

Police photograph of body of Roy Peterson, taken 12:10 A.M.

Police photograph of front coat closet, taken 12:27 A.M.

The closet by the front door where guests' coats were placed on their arrival. We have identified these as belonging to (from left to right): Mabel Hickney, Roy Peterson, Lord Chomley, and Felix Darlington. Vita Simpson arrived with no coat, and Cloris Adder never removed hers. The umbrella on the left belongs to Mabel Hickney. Those in the stand belong to Roy Peterson and Vita Simpson. The one on the floor to the right belongs to Cloris Adder. Lord Chomley's driver held an umbrella for him as he left the car, thus eliminating the need for him to carry his own. Felix Darlington ran from his car to the door without one.

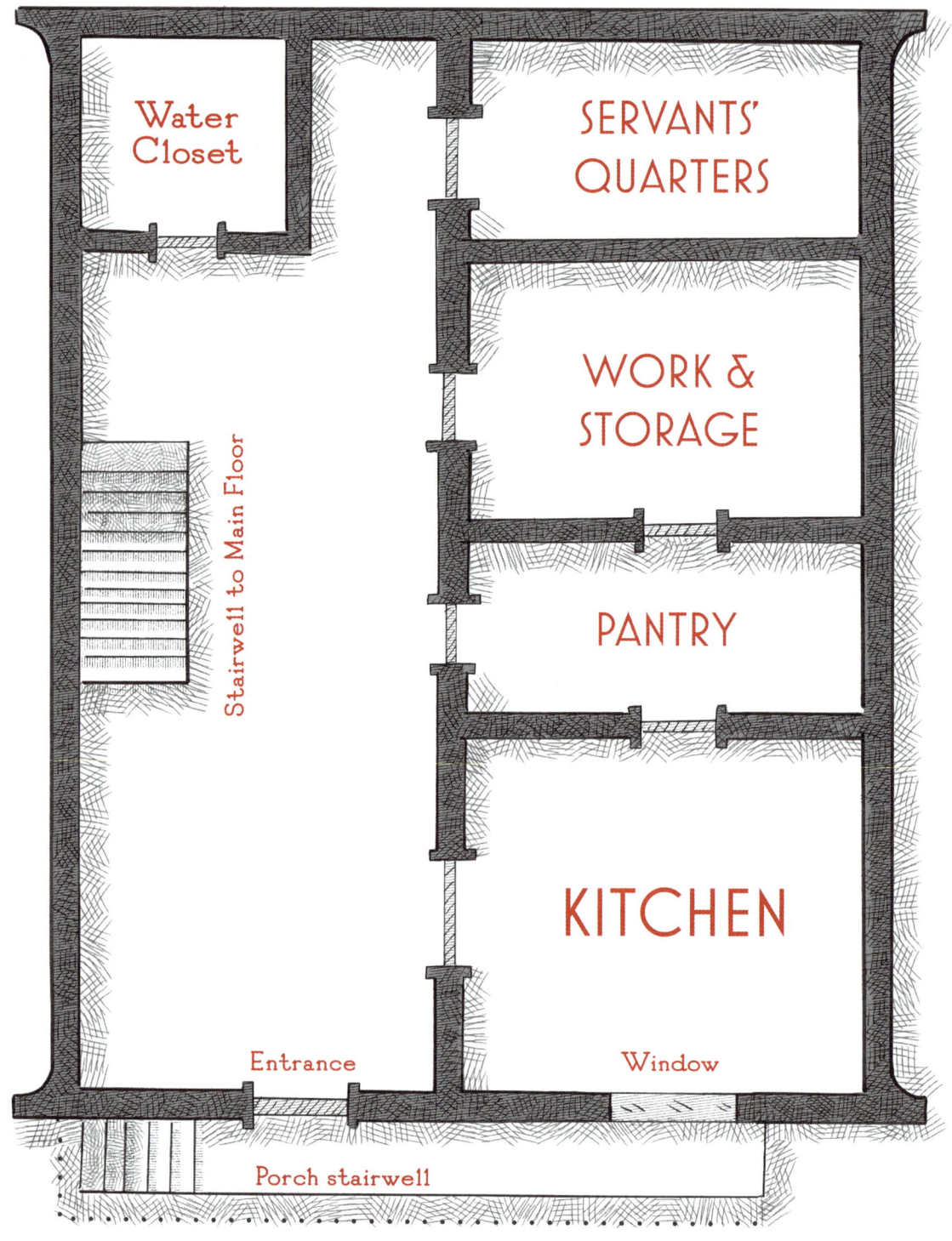

Servants' level, 19 Tootley Row

There are only two means of entry: the door and the window. The door was found locked.
The window had a broken pane by the latch and was slightly open.

Photograph of kitchen, taken 12:25 A.M.
A more complete view of the kitchen door and broken window

Photograph of letter scraps pulled from fire by Constable Wilkins

Photograph of silver container

During the examination of the sitting room, this small silver container was discovered stuffed behind the back cushion of the chair used by Vita Simpson. It was found to contain cocaine. It had been wiped clean of fingerprints.

On the following pages you will find information related to the victim, the witnesses, and the suspects.

You will see mentions of a **Desmond Plott**. Plott was a footman at Lord Chomley's house, Wuthers. Plott got drunk while working during the New Year's Eve party at the end of 1932. He stumbled into a pond on the grounds and drowned. This was ruled a simple accident. However, it is worth noting that all of the suspects were at this party in some capacity or other, as was Billie Snooks. Peterson's letter refers to "the man in the pond." This was the only man in a pond we could find that had connections to the case.

VICTIM

Roy Peterson, age 42, arrived 9:10 P.M.

Obviously, Mr. Peterson could not be interviewed. However, an interview with him had recently been published in the 11 October 1933 issue of the *New York Weekly Magazine*. I have included it to give some background information and a sense of his character.

SUSPECTS PRESENT AT SCENE

Ambrose Belvoir, 29, owner of 19 Tootley Row and poet

Mabel Hickney, 26, telephone operator

Cloris Adder, 58, cook

Felix Darlington, 31, racing driver

Vita Simpson, 27, actress

Lord Alfred Chomley, 65, naturalist

WITNESSES

George Baxter, 27, manservant to Ambrose Belvoir

Edward Finsdale, 48, tailor

Bernard Wells, 59, headwaiter at Gibbons Restaurant

Poison pen letter found in Roy Peterson's coat pocket

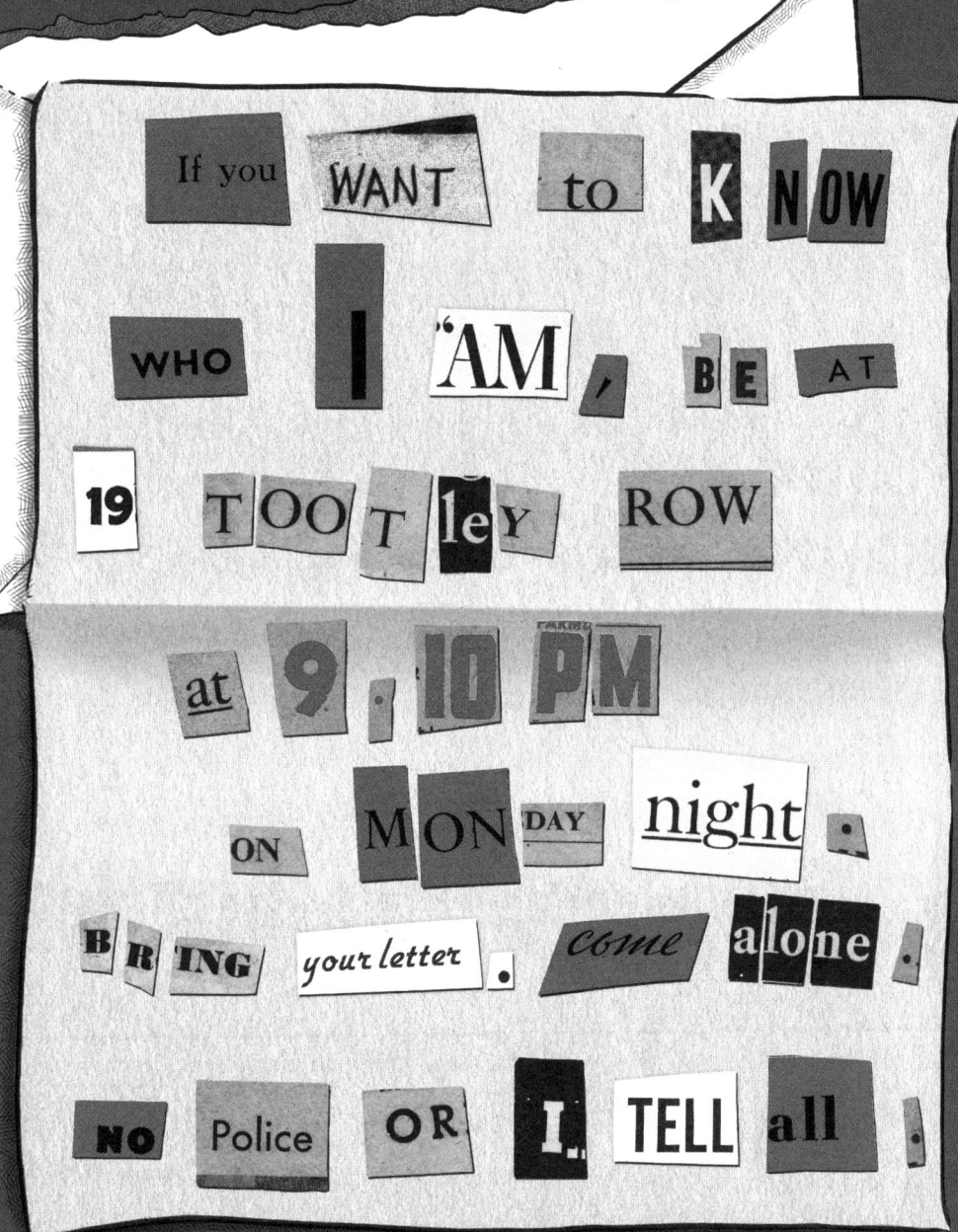

Note found in Roy Peterson's coat pocket

HENDERSON'S CAN'T
AN INTERVIEW WITH ROY PETERSON

BY OONA TORSDALE

ROY PETERSON

Roy Peterson resides on a narrow street in the Soho area of London, behind a bruise-green door with a large black knob in the center. He does not often grant interviews, but had accepted my offer, perhaps thinking no one would come all the way from New York to speak to him. When informed that I would be happy to do so and would be on the next boat, the response was not enthusiastic. I'd been told to come precisely on time. "Do not be late," his editor had told me. "But for the love of god, don't be early either."

It has been five years since the reading public was electrified by the appearance of *Henderson's Can*. It was not Roy Peterson's first novel; it was his third. His first two—*This and Also This* and *Speak Not for the Corn*—were admired by a small set. But then the world read the story of Henry Henderson, a man who falls in love with the daughter of a sardine canning factory owner. When the owner rejects Henderson as a suitable mate for his daughter, Henderson sneaks into the factory to be closer to her. He falls into madness, building a burrow in the machinery and burning the factory down, killing his beloved. The book is perhaps most famous for the last eleven pages, which are comprised entirely of punctuation marks.

The literary world was torn asunder by the book, with some proclaiming it to be the greatest work of the age. "Peterson is a giant among men of letters," claimed one writer. "I have set down my pencil. There is nothing left to be said. I bow low before a master." But not everyone was charmed. One critic enigmatically remarked, "American literature has certainly entered a new era." Another titan of criticism said of it, "I don't know how *Henderson's Can* made it to print. Did someone lose a bet?"

Peterson occupies a small, tidy house, clinically furnished in the Bauhaus style. I followed him into a sitting room, where a pleasant fire burned in a green-tiled fireplace, over which was a pencil sketch of a woman composed of squares falling off what I think was the moon. He took a seat on one of the highly structured chairs. I was not offered a seat but took one anyway. He gazed at me with barely veiled dismay as I took out my notebook, pencil, and cigarettes. As I did so, cats seemed to creep out of every shadow to have a look at me. I decided to start the conversation casually, to get the atmosphere warmed up.

"You've been in London for a while now?" I said. "Over a year?"

"Long enough."

That wasn't a clear answer, but I continued on as if it were.

"Do you prefer the English literary community to the American one?"

"Do you call two or three actual writers making their way among the throng of pedestrian, jobbing pencil-wranglers a literary community?"

"I suppose I do," I said.

"I prefer it here," he replied. "The weather suits me. The people have a sense of order and deference. There is history here. There is a sense of where you are. There are people as well, I suppose. In the arts."

"Who do you keep company with?"

"Thinkers. Artists. Drinkers."

One of the many cats that wandered the floor—a marmalade one of tremendous size—jumped up on the sofa with Peterson. He reached out to tickle its head gently.

"You have a lot of cats," I remarked.

"I have seven."

"That seems a lot."

"Cats," he said, "come and go as they please. They are self-sufficient. They get rid of mice and birds. They do not ask questions."

But interviewers do, and I was an interviewer. It was time to get into the meat of the matter. I opened my notebook. Seeing this, Roy Peterson issued forth a barbed sigh and went to the drinks cart. He poured himself a concoction of several different spirits and sat back down. Perhaps he sensed I didn't want a cocktail at this early hour. Perhaps he did not care.

"I'd like to start by asking about some of the themes in *Henderson's Can*."

"What about them?"

"Well, fish, for instance. *Henderson's Can* is rife with references to them. Ellen, Henderson's beloved, is associated with salmon. Her father is a monkfish. Gentle Irene is a trout, while the antagonist, Dennis, is a tuna. And of course, the sardine rules over all. What do these fish mean to you, the author?"

Peterson stared at me over the top of his glass. For at least five minutes, he said nothing at all. His gaze was steady, but his eyes had a milky, faraway look to them. One of the cats rubbed against my leg, while another strolled along the mantel, almost knocking over what appeared to be a rather fine porcelain vase. The object hovered on the edge of disaster, but neither Peterson nor I made a move to save it.

"I'll tell you something," he finally replied.

I was ready to hear it.

For the next half hour, instead of answering my question, he savaged at least twenty popular literary darlings. No one was left standing. Not Fitzgerald, not Hemingway, not Dos Passos, not Waugh, not Stein, not Wolfe or Norris or any other writer who had the misfortune of being invoked. That included me, but he either did not realize or did not care that *In the Cool Evening Grass* was my work. It took a tremendous beating.

"You don't seem to have a good opinion of the writing community," I said.

"We've dismissed them. Don't you pay attention?"

"What about the reading community?"

"The public?" He laughed bitterly and got up to refill his drink, this time doubling the quantity. "Have you met the public?"

WITH THE MIRACLE TABLET, "SLUMBERAID," LIFE'S CARES WILL DISSOLVE INTO NOTHING.

The cat on the mantel snaked back the way it had come. As it passed, it knocked the vase to its death. Peterson didn't even turn to look at the wreckage.

"How long are you going to be?" he said. "I must work."

I was growing weary of Roy Peterson, but I had come all the way from America for this interview. I pressed on.

"The last eleven pages of *Henderson's Can* are comprised entirely of punctuation marks."

"Well observed."

"Many people—myself included—have had trouble working out what you intended by this."

"I am not surprised," he replied.

"Perhaps you would be so gracious as to enlighten us," I said. "That we may understand your mastery."

He straightened up at this, seemingly unaware of the intended tone of my remark.

"The novel must go beyond language," he said, leaning out of his chair toward me. "By god, we must get past it."

"But surely novels are based in language?"

"Listen to me . . ." The glass was empty and he was up to fill it again. "I read Flaubert as a child, of course—no adult should read Flaubert, I'm sure you'll agree—and . . ."

He finished one glass while standing at the bar and poured another, all the while talking about moving beyond language. I must confess I was having trouble following his train of thought. He paced the room, moving books, dropping them on the floor, mumbling about runes, complimenting cats, extolling the virtues of the London stage, airing personal grievances against H. L. Mencken, describing the perfect roasted potato, and demanding a return to "the loose wilderness of Poe's loins."

"It is," he said, collapsing into a chair, "a case of triangles. Triangles."

He closed his eyes to consider the triangle. After a minute or so of silence, I gathered up the courage to lean forward and ask, "What is the case of triangles?"

But there was no further knowledge for me to absorb. Roy Peterson had fallen asleep.

Items recovered from the body of Roy Peterson. Lighter and cigarette case found in outer jacket pocket. Theater ticket, note, money, and key to his flat found in inner pocket (on the side where he was stabbed, hence the blood). Of note is the theater ticket—*Seven Sailors and Sister Sally*. Billie Snooks was the star of this production. The crumpled note that reads "I saw wot you done" is written in pencil on ordinary writing paper. No usable fingerprints were found.

Undated photograph of George Baxter

INTERVIEW WITH GEORGE BAXTER
(VALET TO AMBROSE BELVOIR)
28 November, 12:05–12:15 A.M.

Mr. Baxter had been given the evening off and had returned to 19 Tootley Row at 11:50 P.M. to find the police investigation underway. I took him aside for my first interview of the night.

I: Mr. Baxter, how long have you worked for Mr. Belvoir?

GB: Just coming up on two years now, inspector.

I: And in what capacity do you serve?

GB: I am Mr. Belvoir's personal gentleman. I answer the door to callers, lay out Mr. Belvoir's clothes, make light meals, serve drinks, that sort of thing. I don't really cook all that much, as Mr. Belvoir usually has meals prepared at Chez Victor and I simply pop round and get them and serve them. But he is partial to a poached egg and I make quite a good one and you can't transport a poached egg, sir. Would you like a poached egg, inspector?

I: No, thank you, and nothing in the kitchen can be touched.

GB: Mustn't touch the kitchen. Understood, inspector.

I: You were out this evening?

GB: Yes, Mr. Belvoir gave me the evening off.

I: What time was that?

GB: Well, I finished the ironing and put the iron away, and then I changed my clothes . . . I was gone by eight-fifteen, sir.

I: And what did you do?

GB: I had dinner and drinks with a friend at the Green Cat—it's a little restaurant nearby.

I: Did you know the nature of Mr. Belvoir's gathering?

GB: Mr. Belvoir has all sorts of gatherings, sir.

I: This one in particular?

GB: No, sir. He said he had friends coming round. It's not my business to know more.

I: Did you know that Mr. Belvoir has received a poison pen letter?

GB: No, I did not, sir!

I: You seem shocked.

GB: I would hope that Mr. Belvoir would tell me if he had received such a letter. What did it say?

I: I can't go into that, Mr. Baxter.

GB: Of course. But . . . just a hint?

I: No. Did you know Mr. Roy Peterson?

GB: Oh yes. Dreary man, inspector.

I: I'd like you to come with me for a moment, Mr. Baxter.

Mr. Baxter followed me down the servants' stairs to the lower level. I indicated the bedroom.

I: Your room, Mr. Baxter?

GB: Yes.

I: You'll need to gather your things and move them to another room upstairs. Before you do that, have a look at that window there.

GB: It's broken!

I: I take it the window was not broken when you left?

GB: No, sir. I would never leave the house with a broken window.

I: So at eight-fifteen that window was not broken?

GB: Absolutely.

I: You keep these windows locked?

GB: Of course, sir. The house is always locked.

I: Who has keys to this downstairs door?

GB: I do, sir. And Mr. Belvoir. But the key to this downstairs door and the main door is the same.

I: The lock is the same?

GB: Yes, sir. You only need one key. You can open either door with it.

I: And only you and Mr. Belvoir have keys?

GB: Yes, sir.

I: Are there spare keys?

GB: Mr. Belvoir keeps a spare for guests, when people stay the night.

I: And where is that kept?

GB: Mr. Belvoir keeps it, sir.

I: And that's the only one?

GB: Yes, sir. I think so, sir. Unless Mr. Belvoir had another made, but I doubt he would, sir. I do that sort of thing for him.

I: Would any of the people present tonight know about the other key?

GB: I expect so, sir. It's not a secret, the key. Many of the people upstairs now have used it at one time or another.

I: Which people?

GB: Miss Simpson. Mr. Darlington. Lord Chomley. Possibly Mr. Peterson.

I: Miss Hickney?

GB: Heavens, no, sir.

I: So let's review the ways into the house. There are two doors—this downstairs door and the front door. There's one broken basement-level window . . .

GB: No one's getting in through that kitchen window, because it sticks. You can't open it more than a few inches. And no one's getting in the bedroom windows unless they brought a ladder and climbed up the front of the building, but I don't imagine anyone would be able to do that without being seen by absolutely everyone.

I: Quite so. And the sitting room windows were locked?

GB: Oh yes. Locked.

I: Can you identify this item, Mr. Baxter?

```
Mr. Baxter was shown the ice pick
found on the floor.
```

GB: Is that blood?

I: I'm afraid so.

GB: Goodness! Yes, I know it. That's the ice pick from the kitchen. It's part of a set of bar tools with jet handles. A gift from his lordship, I believe. Made in France.

I: Lord Chomley?

GB: Yes, sir.

I: When did you last see it?

GB: Why . . . I suppose, earlier tonight? Mr. Belvoir asked me to fill the ice bucket for the bar, so I broke what little ice we had. It's Monday, sir. We're usually short on ice after the weekend, so there was only a little for the bucket. I put it back in the drawer when I was done. And someone was murdered with it?

I: I'm afraid so.

GB: Will Mr. Belvoir get it back?

I: When our investigations are at an end. But I imagine he'll want to get rid of it.

GB: I imagine he'll have it mounted, sir. A murder! Here! It's awful, of course, sir. Dreadful. Could I . . . see it again?

```
Following this interview, Mr. Baxter
was left with Constable Wilkins
while he packed a change of clothes.
```

Photograph of Ambrose Belvoir taken by artist Morgana Frood sometime in June 1933

Police photograph of Ambrose Belvoir taken at 19 Tootley Row, 28 November 1933, 12:17 A.M.

Poison pen letter received by Ambrose Belvoir during the week before the murder, date unknown

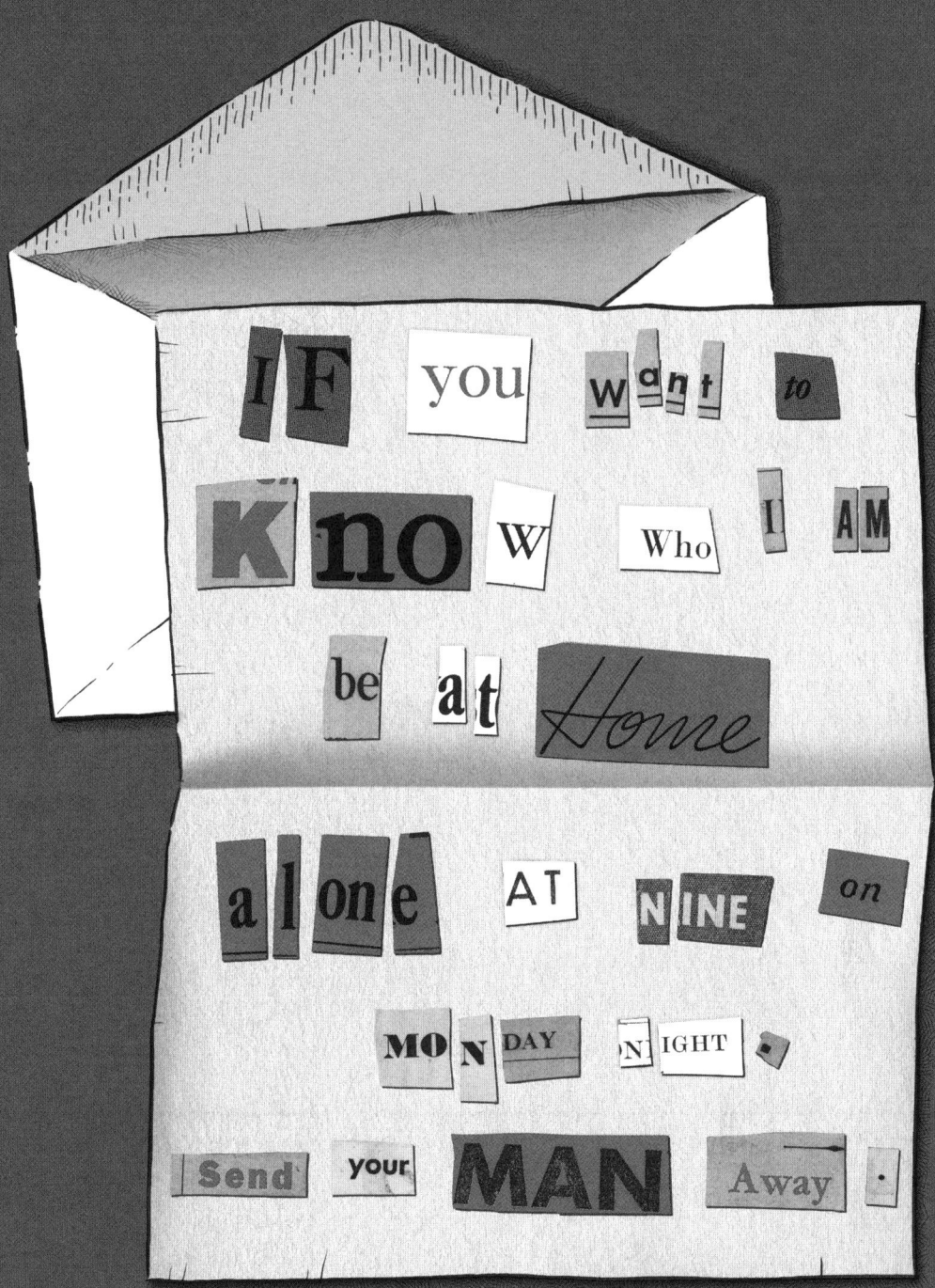

Note received by Ambrose Belvoir on Sunday, 26 November 1933

INTERVIEW WITH AMBROSE BELVOIR

28 November, 12:20–12:30 A.M.

I: Mr. Belvoir, please tell me about the events that led up to the gathering in your house this evening.

AB: Well, as you know, we all received rather naughty little letters. Poison pen, I believe, is the term?

I: Yes. This must have upset you.

AB: On the contrary! I was positively beaming about it! Everyone who's anyone gets a poison pen letter. I'd never gotten one before. I wasn't happy about the content of the letter, but the idea of getting one was delightful.

I: I see. When did you receive your letter?

AB: A week ago. It came in through the mail slot, no stamp. I can't remember which day.

I: You received a second one, about this evening?

AB: Yes. It appeared in the same fashion, right through the mail slot, two days ago. It said to send George away tonight and that at nine o'clock I'd meet the letter writer and find out what was going on. So that is what I did. Sent George off at eight for a lovely evening doing whatever it is he does with his free time. I think he gets up to all sorts. I hear strange noises coming from below the floorboards in here sometimes.

I: Weren't you afraid of letting someone who would send letters like these into your house?

AB: You should see some of the people I let into my house, inspector. I was positively giddy with anticipation. I waited, had a drink, paced to and fro to the window like a ship captain's wife waiting for her beloved to return from the sea. So you can imagine my disappointment when I opened it to find Mabel.

I: Mabel Hickney was the first to arrive?

AB: Yes. At nine o'clock on the button. Rap rap rap on the door, and there she is, damp and dreary, looking like a sad cabbage. She didn't look happy to see me either. She started yelling at me, right there at the door, asking me how dare I send her these terrible letters! I told her I didn't send her anything and to stop shouting. We soon worked out that she had been told to come to my house at a certain hour by the same letter writer. I had no choice but to let her come inside.

I: Had she ever visited you before?

AB: Oh yes, but only with Billie, of course. Poor Billie tried her best to keep her sister entertained. She was a good sister.

I: What happened once she was inside?

AB: Well, she handed me her wet coat and hat for a start. George normally answers the door, so I had to work out that business for myself. She took one of the chairs by the fire. I offered her a drink. Gin and tonic. In November. What can you do? My first thought was that someone was playing a joke on me by sending Mabel my way. Anyway, no sooner had I settled her by the fire then there was another knock at the door. This time, I opened it and found Peterson standing there. I asked him if he'd gotten a letter. He said yes. I invited him in as well.

I: What was his demeanor?

AB: Disgruntled. But less disgruntled than normal. Nearly gruntled, I'd say. Obviously several drinks in, but that was to be expected. I would have called for a doctor if he wasn't.

I: Had he been to your house before?

AB: Many times, but I'm not sure he knew that. I don't think Peterson ever knew where he was after eight in the evening, which is exactly the right attitude, in my opinion.

I: What did he do when he came in? Be as precise as you can be.

AB: I showed him into the sitting room, where Mabel was waiting. He poured himself a drink. A simple whisky, no water, and a lot of it, then set the drink down on the side table next to the chair by the fire. Then he went to the toilet, leaving me once again to make polite conversation with Mabel, who was stewing by the fire and pretending to be interested in a copy of Rimbaud's *Une saison en enfer* that I'd been reading earlier in the evening. Then the door went again, and off I went to answer it. And there on my doorstep was the Adder woman. By this point, I was beginning to feel like Ebenezer Scrooge, with my three ghoulish visitors. After that was Felix, which was a sight for sore eyes. Then my darling Vita, who arrived without a coat because she thought she read somewhere that they're not in this season, bless her. Then Chomley with his graces and airs. There were no more knocks on the door after that until you—I mean the collective you, the police—arrived.

I: And what happened in that hour?

AB: Well, we had all gotten letters, so mostly it was talk of that.

I: What did Roy Peterson say?

AB: Not much, but he wasn't a chatty man. Although . . . he did say something. Something about the ball? Something something ball. I think. He was mumbling. But I know when he said it: 9:35. I was keeping an eye out, you see, for the visiting spirits, so I noted the time, as they seemed to be coming on regular intervals. I had just looked at the clock when Peterson mumbled.

I: Did anyone approach him at any point?

AB: No.

I: You're sure?

AB: I do think I would have noticed if someone walked over and stabbed him with an ice pick.

I: So how did a man who was sitting alone in a chair, approached by no one, get murdered right in front of six other people?

AB: Don't ask me. I'd love to know.

I: You have a spare key for guests?

AB: Yes.

I: Where is it?

AB: Oh, upstairs somewhere. I usually keep it in a little marble pot on the dresser. It's green. Has a gold rim.

```
Constable Wilkins was dispatched to
look for the key, which he located.
```

I: I've seen your letter. It seems to indicate that you gave Billie Snooks, the actress, the cocaine that caused her overdose.

AB: It's a ghastly subject. Billie was my friend. And no, I had nothing to do with it. I did not give Billie cocaine that night.

I: How was Billie Snooks related to this group?

AB: Well, most of us knew her. She was divine, inspector. A delight. A true star. An absolute brick and one of my dearest. She and Vita were good friends. Felix adored her—but I believe she was one of the few women he could not charm into his embrace, if you understand me. Chomley is a friend to all. We often went to his house. Even Peterson melted in her presence. He almost showed tender feelings. How the Adder fits into this I do not know. I've never met that woman before.

I: And Mabel?

AB: Oh goodness, yes. Mabel. Mabel was Billie's sister, as I am sure you know. Poor Billie's death was the best thing that ever happened to her. You should have seen her. You probably did see her. She was in every paper, crying on the front page. Acting runs in the family. She can cry on cue, that one. I've seen her do it. She was charging for interviews. Bereaved sister of dead actress tells tragic story, sister recounts shock cocaine death, that sort of stuff. Horrid. I'm only polite to her because it's what Billie would have wanted, but a pox on her flat.

I: Are you a cocaine user yourself, Mr. Belvoir?

AB: Of course not, inspector.

I: Mr. Belvoir, this is a murder inquiry. I'm not asking because I am interested in your personal habits. I am asking because someone is dead in your sitting room and you have a letter claiming that you gave Billie Snooks the cocaine that killed her. Answer the question.

AB: My goodness, so direct! I'll say this: I have no idea where she got her supply from that dreadful night. Not from me. And Billie had started to take other things. Cocaine brings you up, I'm told. Right to the ceiling. Sometimes it can be hard to get down again. I think she went up, up, up that night and took something else to get back down, and I suspect those things didn't play well together. It can be quite dangerous to mix certain substances. Or so I've heard. But I was not the one who provided it.

I: A small pillbox containing cocaine was found shoved between some cushions this evening.

```
The box was shown to Mr. Belvoir.
```

AB: What a jolly little item that is! Not mine, sadly. And if you really want to know, I gave the stuff up after Billie died.

I: What can you tell me about this, Mr. Belvoir? This was the note we found in Mr. Peterson's pocket.

```
Mr. Belvoir was shown the crumpled
note in Roy Peterson's pocket.
```

AB: *I saw wot you did*. How very cryptic. I assume it has to do with that poor fellow at Chomley's place. Ploot. Plum. Pratt. Good-looking fellow. A footman.

I: There was a man named Desmond Plott who died at Lord Chomley's estate on New Year's Eve.

AB: Plott! That's absolutely what it was—how clever of you. Desmond Plott. Got drunk and fell into an ornamental pond. Very sad. I was there for that party. I know because I've seen the photographs. But I don't remember anything except waking up in London a day or so later. I managed to stay drunk the entire time and someone drove me back. Felix, possibly. I heard that someone had drowned.

I: Why did Roy Peterson have a letter referencing the death of Desmond Plott?

AB: Haven't the slightest. I doubt Roy Peterson had any idea who Desmond Plott was. He didn't strike me as the kind of person who paid particular attention to the people serving him.

I: What else can you tell me about Mr. Peterson?

AB: Have you read *Henderson's Can*?

I: No. I understand it's very good.

AB: Good? It's abysmal. Absolute rot. Five hundred pages about fish. Well, it's about sex, of course. You don't have to be our friend from Vienna to work out what he's talking about when he tries to open that can of sardines . . .

I: Thank you, Mr. Belvoir.

AB: I don't eat fish, myself. It's the bones, you see. Those tiny bones.

I: Thank you.

AB: Once you've read that book, you can understand why someone would want to murder the man. What an absolute wheeze. Naughty boy. And dead in my sitting room, which is rather extraordinary.

I: That will be all for now, Mr. Belvoir. I'm very sorry about what's happened here in your home.

AB: On the contrary. This is the best party I've ever had!

```
NOTE: Mr. Belvoir's pockets were
empty. This is not surprising, given
that he was home and had no need to
carry items he might want, such as
cigarettes or a lighter.
```

Undated photograph of Mabel Hickney

Note received by Mabel Hickney on Monday, 27 November 1933

Poison pen letter received by Mabel Hickney

Police photograph of Mabel Hickney taken at 19 Tootley Row, 28 November 1933, 12:20 A.M.

INTERVIEW WITH MABEL HICKNEY

28 November, 12:35–12:45 A.M.

I: Miss Hickney, tell me about the events that led up to this evening. You received a poison pen letter. When was that?

MH: About . . . about a week or so ago. Oh yes. It was Tuesday. I remember because I was going to my hairdresser that day.

I: And how did it arrive?

MH: Through the mail slot. But it didn't have a stamp. Someone must have hand-delivered it. I thought it was a note from a friend, so I opened it without thinking and, oh, it was so horrible!

I: You got another note telling you to come here tonight at nine?

MH: Yes. To 19 Tootley Row. I knew the address, of course.

I: You're a friend of Mr. Belvoir?

MH: He and my sister were close. I'd come with her. But I am not a friend of his. Of any of that lot. Those fiends—those absolute fiends—got her involved with cocaine. That whole set. Ambrose, Vita, Felix, Chomley. They killed my sister.

I: When did this second note arrive?

MH: This morning. It was there when I woke up. I've recently moved to a darling little place near Bloomsbury, and my maid brought it up for me.

I: You live at 57 Stankton Place, I believe. You are a lodger at the home of Mrs. Ethel Crancook, is that correct?

MH: Well, yes. It's so snug and cozy. It reassures me to live with someone else. And she cleans, of course.

I: Of course. How did you get here this evening?

MH: Well, I was going to get a taxi but I just couldn't seem to find one, so I took the bus.

I: Did you get off at the stop at the end of the road?

MH: Yes.

I: And you got off the bus at what time?

MH: Eight-fifteen.

I: That left you with forty-five minutes in the pouring rain. What did you do?

MH: I went to the Lyons' Corner House for a cup of tea. To calm my nerves.

I: So you had tea at the Lyons', and left there at what time?

MH: Eight forty-five.

I: It's about a ten-minute walk from the Lyons' to here, I'd say.

MH: Yes. About that. I was a few minutes early, so I just paced about a bit and rang the door at nine. Ambrose answered. I may have yelled at him. I thought he'd sent the letter, but he soon assured me that he hadn't. So I came inside. He took my coat, and I went through to the sitting room.

I: Was anyone there?

MH: No. I sat near the fire, as I was cold. Ambrose offered me a drink. He said he'd gotten a letter saying he'd killed my sister! He wanted to know what mine said, but I didn't show it to him. Then someone else knocked on the door. I assumed it was the letter writer, but then in came Roy. Dear, sweet Roy.

I: You were friends?

MH: Oh yes. He was encouraging me to write a book about my sister. A good man. And brilliant! Have you read his book, *Henderson's Can*?

I: I have not.

MH: You should. It's a work of genius.

I: I'll make a note to do so. What did Mr. Peterson do? How did he seem?

MH: Quiet. He took the other chair by the fire, so we were quite far apart. He got a drink. Then he excused himself.

I: To do what?

MH: I believe he needed to use the . . . toilet.

I: I see. The one in the hall?

MH: Yes.

I: So you were alone again with Mr. Belvoir?

MH: Only for a moment. I tried to ignore him and read a book. I was going to wait until Roy came back to talk. But then someone else knocked at the door. Ambrose went out. Roy came back in and sat down.

I: And how did he seem then?

MH: Fine. He took a long sip of his drink. Ambrose came in with a woman I've never met before and said, "This is Mrs. Cloris Adder." And then something about ghosts.

I: And she sat where?

MH: On the sofa, the one next to Roy. She didn't say anything. Just sat there looking a bit like a frog.

I: Where did Mr. Belvoir sit?

MH: He didn't, really. He perched on the backs of chairs and was saying all kinds of inane things about how he thought the evening was going, and then there was the door again, and in came Felix Darlington. Who is a very bad man indeed, inspector.

I: In what way?

MH: In the . . . classical way.

I: The classical way?

MH: With . . . women.

I: I see. A lothario.

MH: Yes. That. He was in love with my sister, but she brushed him off. Billie was too good for the likes of him. He doesn't like me because of it.

I: I see. So, what happened then?

MH: Cloris Adder started demanding to know what was going on, Ambrose said he didn't know but was excited to find out. No one knew what was going on. And then, another knock, and there was Vita. I'd been there a while and people were just coming and coming. Vita said hello to me. I said hello, for my sister's sake. Then, ten minutes later, another knock and that horrid Chomley came in, yelling about getting a letter. We waited, but no one else came.

I: Did everyone else talk about the contents of their letters?

MH: No. Only Ambrose, who seemed to be enjoying himself.

I: Did Mr. Peterson speak at all?

MH: Roy said something at some point, but he wasn't terribly clear. About a ball? I believe he was rather intoxicated. And then he seemed to fall asleep.

I: Did you see anyone go near Mr. Peterson?

MH: No. No! He was just sitting there! No one was anywhere near him!

I: Did you see anything around his seat? You would have had a clear view from across the fire.

MH: You mean that ice pick? No, but I wasn't looking under his chair.

I: Do you know if anyone in the room had any problem with Roy Peterson?

MH: No. I don't think anyone did. But I don't know Cloris Adder or how she fit in with everything.

I: So when the constable came, that's when you realized Mr. Peterson was dead?

MH: Yes.

I: And what did you do?

MH: I don't know. I jumped up, I suppose. We all did. Oh, it was horrible. Oh . . .

`MH wept for some moments.`

MH: I can go on. I can go on.

I: Very good. Now, your sister was Billie Snooks, the actress.

`MH began weeping again.`

MH: Yes. Billie was my sister. That wasn't her real name, of course. Her real name was Doris Hickney. She needed something more glamorous. Many people change their name for the stage.

I: I understand. And your sister passed away from a drug overdose.

`MH began weeping again.`

MH: It's all right. I can go on. Yes. It's true. They did it to her. They got her involved with cocaine!

I: *They* being . . .

MH: Ambrose. Vita. Chomley. Felix.

I: Not Mr. Peterson?

MH: Mr. Peterson did not use cocaine!

I: How do you know this?

MH: He simply wouldn't!

I: I see. Now, your letter—take my handkerchief, Miss Hickney—your letter claims you disliked your sister.

MH: Lies! Terrible lies! My sister was an angel!

I: And quite famous.

MH: Oh yes.

I: Glamorous.

MH: Oh yes.

I: What is your profession, Miss Hickney?

MH: I am a telephone operator.

I: A most respectable profession. But not as glamorous as your sister's, to be fair.

MH: Of course not, but . . . Billie took me everywhere. All the parties. The nightclubs. Most of them, anyway. Quite a lot of them. And she let me wear her clothes. She was a darling younger sister.

I: When she died, you gave many interviews.

MH: Yes. To talk about how wonderful she was!

I: You gave personal details in some of those interviews, Miss Hickney. About the clubs and the parties.

MH: Yes, of course. There's nothing wrong with that.

I: And you spoke of the drugs she took.

MH: Everyone knew, inspector. She had died of an overdose.

I: Quite so.

MH: And I also wanted the world to know of the evils of those drugs.

I: Commendable. Were you paid for this public service?

MH: I . . . received small fees now and again.

I: I see. Now, one more thing, Miss Hickney. You have a book of matches from Gibbons Restaurant in your bag.

MH: Yes.

I: Do you frequent Gibbons?

MH: I've been there once or twice.

I: Recently?

MH: Perhaps a week or so ago?

I: You weren't there this evening?

MH: No.

I: Very good. That should be all for now.

MH: Do you think this will be in all the papers tomorrow?

I: We'll try our best to keep reporters away, Miss Hickney.

MH: Oh. Oh, yes. Of course. How kind. But you mustn't worry about me when you have a case to solve.

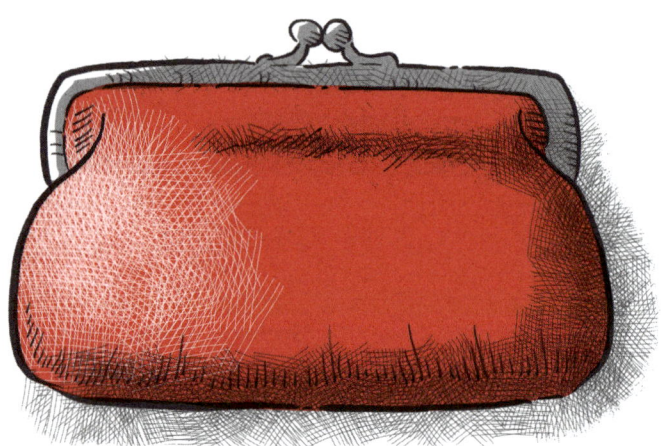

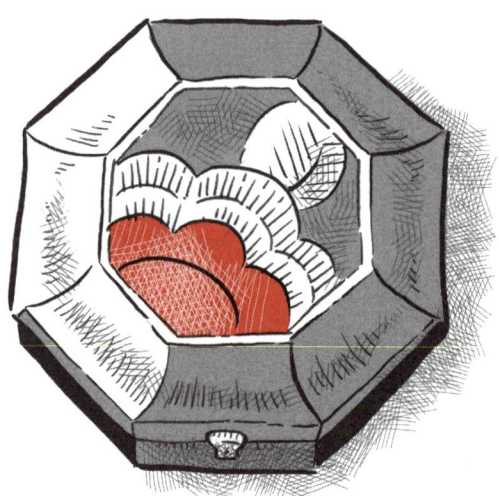

Contents of Mabel Hickney's purse. Clockwise from top left: coin purse containing a small amount of money, keys to the front door and personal door of her flat in the lodging house, silver cigarette case, bus ticket, telephone-and-address book and pencil, matchbook from Gibbons, lipstick, card for an editor at the *Squeaker* newspaper, powder compact. We went through the addresses and found information for Vita Simpson, Lord Chomley, Ambrose Belvoir, and Felix Darlington.

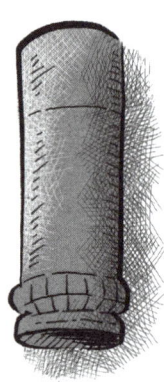

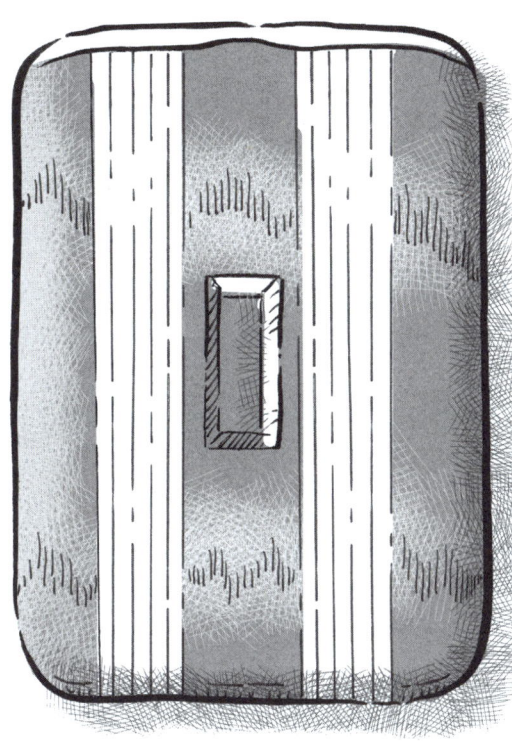

Undated photograph of Cloris Adder

Police photograph of Cloris Adder taken at 19 Tootley Row, 28 November 1933, 12:18 A.M.

Poison pen letter received by Cloris Adder

Note received by Cloris Adder on Monday, 27 November 1933

INTERVIEW WITH CLORIS ADDER

28 November, 1:10–1:20 A.M.

I: Mrs. Adder, I need to ask you . . .

CA: No you bloody well don't.

I: Pardon?

CA: You don't need to ask me nothing. This is all for the bloody papers, innit?

I: Mrs. Adder, this is a police matter. A man has been killed.

CA: Nothing to do with me.

I: Mrs. Adder, you were present in a room where a man was stabbed to death.

CA: I didn't see no stabbing. In the old days, we kept ourselves to ourselves. We did our jobs.

I: Mrs. Adder!

CA: What?

I: You are obligated, in the name of the law, to answer my questions.

CA: Why didn't you say that?

I: Mrs. Adder, I need you to tell me the events that led to your presence at 19 Tootley Row this evening.

CA: That's personal.

I: Not in a murder inquiry. We already have your letter, Mrs. Adder, and we've gone through your purse.

CA: What!

I: Every person here has been subjected to the same, including Lord Chomley. You have not been singled out. And you will sit here until you answer my questions to my satisfaction. Do you understand?

CA: Yes.

I: We are perfectly clear?

CA: Yes.

I: Then let's try this one more time. You are the cook at the London residence of Lady Quisper-Shores, who resides at 89 Devingsham Square?

CA: Yes.

I: How long have you been in her employment?

CA: Five months.

I: And where were you employed before that?

CA: At Wuthers in Gloucester.

I: That's Lord Alfred Chomley's house, is it not?

CA: Yes.

I: And why did you leave there?

CA: Wanted to be closer to my sister here in London is all.

I: I see. We know you received a poison pen letter and then a note telling you to be here this evening. Tell us when and how you received these notes.

CA: They came in the post.

I: Were they stamped?

CA: First one was.

I: And when did that arrive?

CA: A week ago.

I: And the note telling you to be here tonight?

CA: This morning. No stamp, just came through the door and got sent down to me.

I: Good. Now we're getting somewhere. The people who are here tonight—you knew Lord Chomley, of course.

CA: I worked for his lordship. Doesn't mean I know him.

I: What about the others?

CA: They came round to Wuthers, the lot of them. Scandalous lot. Horrid.

I: Did you ever have personal interactions with any of them in your work capacity?

CA: No.

I: Fine. Now, what time did you arrive here this evening?

CA: The note said to come at 9:20 so I came at 9:20. I know my timing. I'm a cook. Everything I do is on time. Never served a cold meal that was meant to be hot.

I: And how did you get here?

CA: Took the bus.

I: Who answered the door?

CA: That fellow in the green. Belfast.

I: Mr. Belvoir.

CA: If you say so.

I: I do. What happened then?

CA: Gave him a piece of my mind for sending me such . . .

I: Such?

CA: I never served no one no bad meat. I never buy cheap meat! I use my food budget right and to the penny. I can get a good deal, though, they all knows me, the fishmonger, the butcher, the fruit-and-veg man. They all know Cloris. I buy good food and cook it proper and all my employers say so, you ask them. You ask them about Cloris's roast joint or duck breast. You ask them who cooks their asparagus better than Cloris.

I: You took exception to the letter?

CA: I never! Never. Do you hear me? My masters and mistresses love what I cooks for them. The staff gets what they get, but I do my best with that as well, and I run a tight kitchen and no foolery downstairs.

I: I see. So you yelled at Mr. Belvoir?

CA: He told me he didn't write the letter, that he got one himself, come inside, so I come inside.

I: Who was there?

CA: This woman Mabel sitting by the fire, looking smug. And that drunken-mess writer already had the other seat by the fire. No seat by the fire for me, so I sat on the sofa, and I waited for an explanation. The man, Belvoir, offered me a drink but I don't drink except at Christmas, and then I sat and waited to find out what was going on, but it was all waiting and mumbling about letters. I wondered if they were playing at something.

I: How did Mr. Peterson seem?

CA: Like I said, drunk.

I: Did he say anything?

CA: Just mumbled a bit. Mostly it was the Belvoir one going on about ghosts and how much fun he was having. Then the tall one came, Felix. You can tell he's a bad one. Then the blond woman, empty-headed, without even the sense to wear a coat, and then his lordship, and he's a . . .

I: A what? What about his lordship?

CA: Nothing. I ain't saying nothing. I don't talk about former employers. A good servant keeps their mouth shut.

I: But you are not a servant now, Mrs. Adder. You are both a suspect and a witness.

CA: Suspect?

I: Yes. Which means that you do talk. About anyone. The law demands it. You worked at Wuthers, Lord Chomley's estate. You were there when a footman named Desmond Plott drowned on New Year's Eve.

CA: Plott was a shiftless layabout who should have been sacked ten times over. I told Spoonworth and he said . . .

I: Who is Spoonworth?

CA: His lordship's butler. Spoonworth said he knew Plott was no good but his lordship liked him. You need them tall and good-looking to be footmen. Plott thought he was better than everyone else.

I: What do you know about his death on New Year's Eve?

CA: Got drunk and drowned is what he did. Good riddance.

I: What about Roy Peterson? Do you think he knew Desmond Plott?

CA: Why would he?

I: Is that a yes or a no?

CA: Plott was staff. Mr. Peterson was a guest. That's all I know.

I: And did you know Mr. Peterson before tonight?

CA: He was a guest at Wuthers. He's a writer.

I: Did you see anyone approach Mr. Peterson tonight?

CA: No. We was all sat talking. Some got drinks but the drinks was on the other side of the room. No. He sat there drunk and then he was dead and I can't tell you more than that. I still don't know who sent me this note, but it's late and I'll have to wait ages for a night bus.

I: We can take you home in a police vehicle when we are through, Mrs. Adder.

CA: Oh? Well, that's very kind of you, inspector. I don't ride in automobiles often. Very nice. I'll give you a slice of my apple cake when we get back. Everyone knows my apple cake.

Contents of Cloris Adder's purse. Clockwise from top left: keys to her London home and workplace, along with one spare key from Wuthers; bus ticket; change purse containing just under two pounds in coins; a folding pocketknife; a box of matches; and a safety pin.

Undated photograph of Felix Darlington

Police photograph of Felix Darlington taken at 19 Tootley Row, 28 November 1933, 12:19 A.M.

Poison pen letter received by Felix Darlington

Note received by Felix Darlington on Sunday, 26 November 1933

INTERVIEW WITH FELIX DARLINGTON

28 November, 1:40–1:50 A.M.

I: Mr. Darlington, please do take a seat.

FD: Yes. Of course. A seat. Yes!

I: Yes. I'm going to ask you some questions, Mr. Darlington.

FD: Ask away!

I: You seem very chipper despite having just been at the scene of a murder, Mr. Darlington.

FD: Murder. Of course. I'll play along!

I: I beg your pardon?

FD: Ambrose almost got me for a moment back there. Almost thought the blighter was dead.

I: This is no trick, I assure you. Roy Peterson is dead.

FD: That can't be a real moustache. Should have spotted it right away . . .

```
Mr. Darlington reached for my
moustache and began pulling it.
Constable Wilkins restrained Mr.
Darlington's arm.
```

I: That's enough! Sit down, Mr. Darlington!

FD: So this is all real? This seems like the sort of thing Ambrose might do for fun, you understand. Roy's dead?

I: He is. And I'd like to understand how that came to pass. Can you tell me when you received your poison pen letter?

FD: Oh, a week ago. My man brought it in with my post. You're supposed to put them in the fire, aren't you? But I put it away in a drawer, didn't think of it again, and then I got the note telling me to be here tonight, and I thought, dash it, I want to see the blighter. And it was Ambrose's address, which was dashed odd.

I: When did you receive this second note?

FD: Yesterday morning.

I: So you arrived at what time tonight?

FD: Nine-thirty, like my letter said. Had to drive a bit on the fast side to make it on time. I drive an SS 1 in town. It's a corker!

I: What happened after your arrival?

FD: Well, Ambrose answered the door, which was dashed odd. I came inside to find Mabel, and Roy half asleep, and some angry sort of person perched on one of the sofas. Got a drink. Sat down. Made conversation.

I: What did you talk about?

FD: The letters we'd gotten. The woman on the sofa—called Adder, I believe—was complaining. Mabel looked angry enough to burst. Ambrose seemed to be having a wonderful time. Roy said nothing.

I: Nothing?

FD: Oh, hang on a moment. He did say something. Mumbled. Something about a hole.

I: A hole?

FD: Honestly, I couldn't tell you for sure.

I: Did anyone approach Mr. Peterson at all?

FD: No. He was off by himself, half asleep. Peterson is a bit of an old stick. Most Americans I meet are jolly enough, though they work too much. Peterson always looked like he'd just bitten the wormy part of the apple. Always banging on about books. No interest in cars at all, or horses, or cricket. And you didn't want to be around him at the end of the night. Twelve drinks in is usually when he'd start eating the furniture. Still. Dead and whatnot. But no. On my life, no one went near him.

I: About your letter, Mr. Darlington. It indicates that you may have been involved in a serious accident.

FD: Well, who hasn't? It wasn't my fault, anyway. He wandered into the road.

I: Who did?

FD: The old fella. It was after the Fairy Lights Ball at Bluenose Hall a year or so ago. I was coming back to London in my Zipawae Model S. The 1929. Remarkable car. I could get her up to a hundred in second gear, and that was without the supercharger! I took it with me to America and overtook a Duesenberg outside of New York! Fantastic stuff.

I: About the accident, Mr. Darlington.

FD: Yes, that's the thing. I was tooling along at a lovely seventy miles per on a clear spring morning on a country road, nothing but blue skies ahead of me and the engine purring like an absolute lion, when out of the hedgerow leaps this man. Just springs right into the road and into my Zipawae. Got her repaired, but she was never the same.

I: Neither was the man.

FD: Well, no, I expect not, after the dent he made in the Zipawae. Nothing I could do, inspector. Walked right in front of the car. Can't help a thing like that.

I: I have another question. Some of the letters received were about Billie Snooks, the actress. You have a picture of Miss Billie Snooks in your wallet.

FS: Yes. Yes, I do.

I: Why is that?

FS: Because we were in love. Dash it, it's hard to talk about, inspector.

I: I see. So you were in love with Billie Snooks?

FD: Yes. We would have married. She was so beautiful, so spry and delightful. Such good fun. Everyone loved her. Even Peterson fell under her spell, and he seemed made of stone.

I: These other pictures in your wallet are . . .

FD: Oh, you know, inspector. Sweethearts of mine since Billie passed.

I: And there's a bit of a phone number on this matchbook. May I ask whose number this is?

```
I handed the matchbook to Mr.
Darlington.
```

FD: Oh yes. Forgot I had this. Had a jolly time at the Gargoyle Club some weeks ago. Met a lovely girl named Felicia. Must telephone her.

I: And you were at Lord Chomley's New Year's Eve party, were you not?

FD: Yes. I was.

I: A man died that night. Were you aware of it?

FD: Oh, yes. Funny business. Man drowned. Got drunk, I believe, wandered out and fell into the pond. Billie was crushed. She had such a tender heart.

I: The man's name was Desmond Plott.

FD: Was it? Sounds right.

I: Did you know him?

FD: I think he was a footman? Something like that?

I: That's correct.

FD: That's all I know, I'm afraid. Billie was beside herself and wanted to come back to London, and Vita, too. Ambrose was absolutely blotto. I packed them all in my car and drove home.

I: Do you recognize this item?

```
Mr. Darlington was shown the closed
cocaine container.
```

FD: Not mine. Not my sort of style.

I: You have been around several deaths, Mr. Darlington. The man on the road, the footman, now Roy Peterson.

FD: Yes, well, that's life, isn't it, inspector? Funny old thing. Really, though, that moustache is real? Extraordinary.

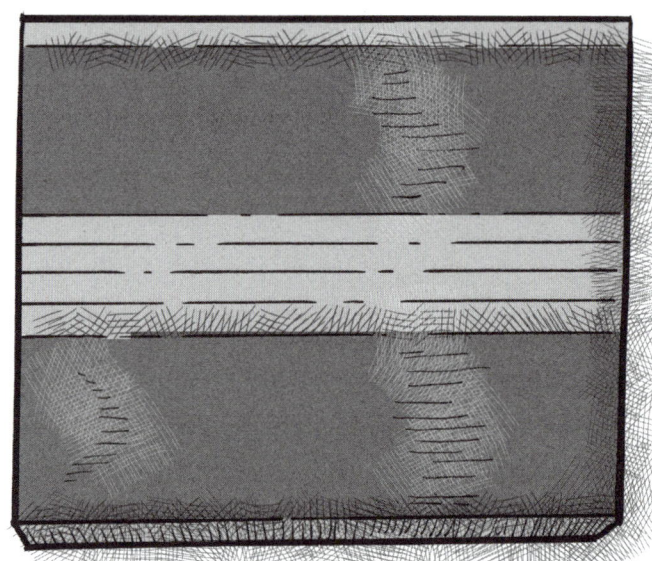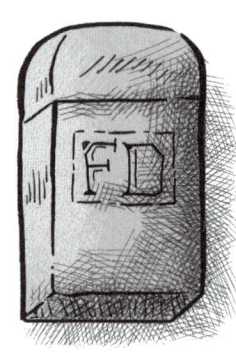

Contents of Felix Darlington's pockets. Clockwise from top left: cigarette case and lighter, wallet, door key, car key, matchbook with section of phone number, photographs of three women—two found to be unrelated to this matter, and one of Billie Snooks.

Undated publicity photograph of Vita Simpson

Police photograph of Vita Simpson taken at 19 Tootley Row, 28 November 1933, 12:21 A.M.

Poison pen letter received by Vita Simpson

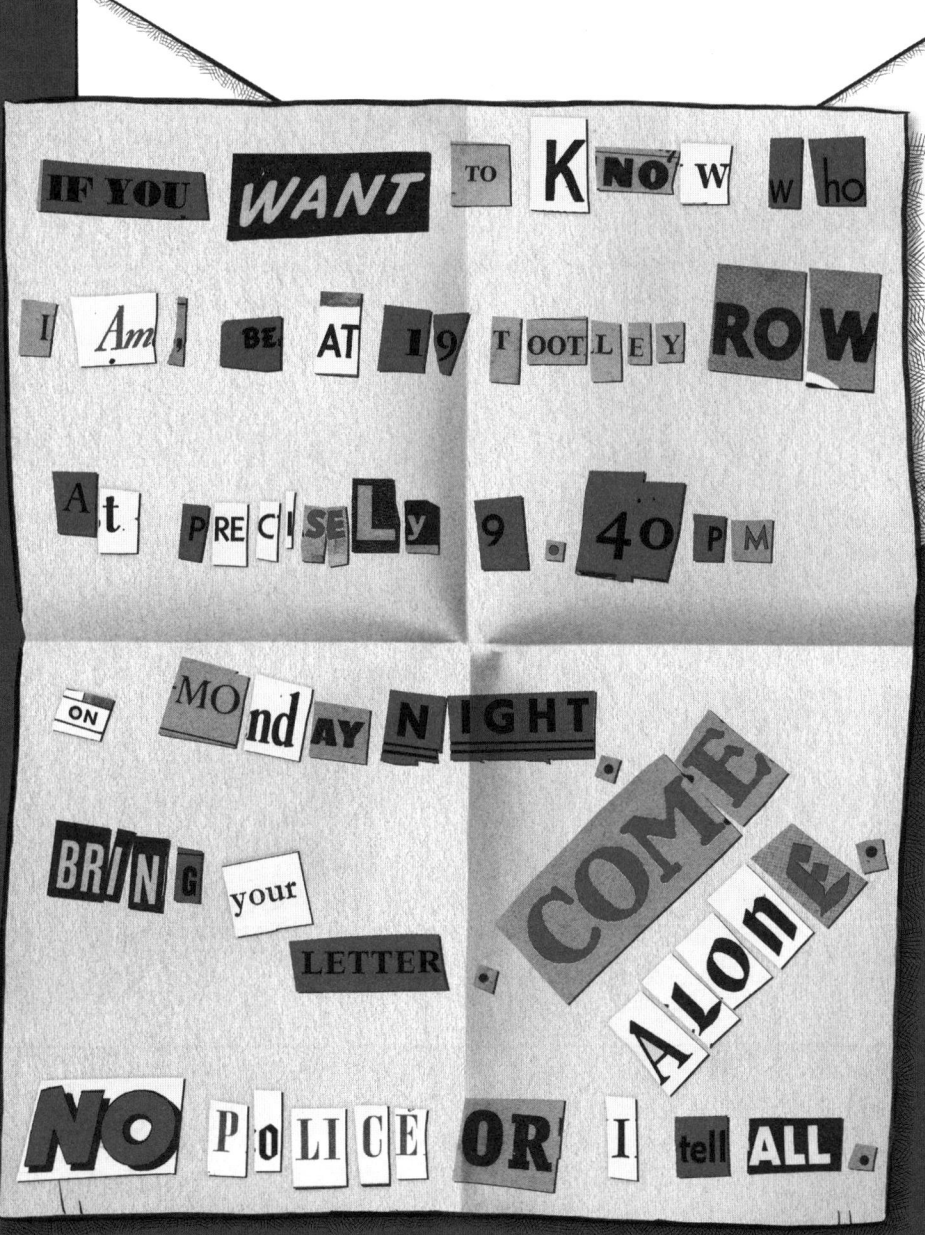

Note received by Vita Simpson on Sunday, 26 November 1933

INTERVIEW WITH VITA SIMPSON

28 November, 12:50–1:00 A.M.

I: Please sit down, Miss Simpson.

VS: All right. Thank you, inspector. I wasn't sure if I had to stand in front of you.

I: No. I am not a judge, Miss Simpson. Please. Sit. Now, I need to ask you some questions about the things that led us to tonight, and the night itself.

VS: About Roy.

I: Yes. Among other things.

VS: He is dead, isn't he, inspector?

I: Yes, I'm afraid so.

VS: Poor Roy. Who killed him?

I: That's what we're here to find out. You are all both witnesses and suspects.

VS: Witness and suspects? Oh. I hope it wasn't me. I'm sure I would have known. I have an excellent memory, inspector. I know all my lines, always. Sometimes I know the other actresses' lines and if they don't say them I'll say them for them. It's most helpful.

I: I'm sure it is. You are an actress?

VS: Yes. Have you seen me? I'm not in a show right now but I've been in loads of shows. Would you like a ticket to one when I get my next one?

I: No thank you, Miss Simpson. Now, can you tell me about your letters? When did you receive the first one?

VS: Oh. Yes. That one made me so very sad. It came about a week ago.

I: Was it stamped?

VS: No. It just came through the door with the post and I read it and . . .

Vita Simpson took a moment to collect herself.

VS: It was about my friend Billie, you see. She died of an overdose.

I: The second note, the one that told you to be here tonight. When did you get it?

VS: Sunday morning. My maid brought it in with my tea. She said someone had put it through the door. It told me to come here, to Ambrose's. I'm always here at Ambrose's, so I wondered if Ambrose was playing a trick or something, but I came when it said to come. I wanted to know who was saying such terrible things. The letter made me so sad.

I: Tell me about your arrival.

VS: Well, Ambrose answered the door, which he never does! And he said, "Where's your coat, darling?" And I explained that Lorna Fitzwapple told me that coats are out for the season. But now that I think of it Lorna once said shoes were out for the season and I went to the Savoy barefoot so maybe Lorna was playing a trick on me. So many people play tricks on me, but it's all in good fun!

I: Of course.

VS: I came inside and there was a party of sorts going on. Felix was there, and Mabel, and Roy, and a strange little woman I didn't know. And it turns out that we'd all gotten letters, inspector! And we were all waiting for the person who wrote them. And then there was a knock at the door, and there was dear Alfred . . .

I: Lord Chomley.

VS: Yes, and he'd gotten a letter as well! So I felt a bit better, as we were all sad about our letters.

I: How did Mr. Peterson seem?

VS: Sleepy. He barely said a word and then he nodded off, except he didn't, did he, inspector. He died!

I: Yes.

VS: Which is a kind of nodding off, I suppose.

I: Did you go anywhere near him or see anyone near him?

VS: Oh, no. He was quite alone. How did it happen, the stabbing? Ambrose spoke of ghosts. I'm quite afraid of ghosts.

I: Mr. Peterson was not stabbed by a ghost, I can assure you.

VS: That does make me feel a bit better.

I: You knew the other people, aside from the woman named Cloris Adder?

VS: Oh yes! Ambrose is my dearest friend, and there's Mabel, who was my friend Billie's sister. And Roy. He's quite brilliant. And Felix, who's a rascal, if I'm being honest, inspector.

I: You must be honest.

VS: It sounds so unkind, but Felix *is* a rascal.

I: In what way?

VS: Oh, he's broken so many hearts! And of course there is dear Albert, who always has us for the weekend and throws such lovely parties. He's famous for them!

I: He had an employee named Desmond Plott. Did you know him?

VS: The footman. Yes. He died. He seemed lovely. He drowned in the pond on New Year's Eve. It seemed like no one cared. He was just taken away and everyone acted like nothing had happened, but I was sad and I took some flowers from one of the vases down to the pond and put them in. It seemed so odd for him to drown like that.

I: Did something seem suspicious?

VS: Well, yes. How odd to drown in a little pond. I fell into a pond once, inspector, but I didn't drown. I climbed out. I ruined my hat, though. It was a lovely Elsa Schiaparelli made of black fur and trimmed in silver satin. I thought it was strange that he didn't just get out of the pond.

I: I see. Let's leave that for now and get to the subject of your letter.

VS: Billie.

I: Yes.

VS: She was my friend, inspector.

I: You cared for her?

VS: With all my heart.

I: Is the letter true? Did you give her the cocaine that killed her?

VS: No. I didn't. But I must be honest, mustn't I? I have used cocaine, inspector. I know it's wrong. I don't anymore. But I did introduce her to it. And I feel so dreadful all the time about it. I miss her.

I: I am very sorry for your loss. A question about Billie—do you know if she had a relationship with Felix Darlington?

VS: Billie didn't like Felix.

I: Why was that?

VS: As I said, inspector, he can be charming but he's awfully careless about people. Do you know what I mean?

I: I think I do. You mean he breaks hearts.

VS: He does. I think he was a bit in love with Billie, but Billie didn't like him. She was too good for that. She was lovely, inspector. A lovely person.

I: So they didn't have a relationship?

VS: No. They did not.

I: Forgive my asking, but have you had a relationship with Mr. Darlington?

VS: No. And not for his lack of trying. The last time he mentioned it, I threw a banana at him. Is that illegal, inspector?

I: I think we can overlook the banana, Miss Simpson. Now, this container was found in your chair this evening, stuffed between the cushions.

```
Miss Simpson was shown the
container and the cocaine
inside.
```

VS: That's not mine, inspector. When I used cocaine I carried it in a small green box. I've thrown that away.

I: I see. Can you tell me anything else you saw that might be of any help? Anything at all?

VS: Let me think. When the constable came, we were all in an uproar. Alfred was doing something odd by the fire. I went over to look and he tried to distract me, but I knew what he was doing, inspector. I'm not as silly as people think I am. I saw him throw something in the fire. And the constable saw him, too, and got it out. It was Alfred's letter.

I: That's very good to know, Miss Simpson. Was there anything else?

VS: No. I'm just so frightened. Roy was stabbed! Right in front of us! I know you said it's not ghosts but it could be ghosts. Lorna once told me she saw a ghost steal my cigarettes and when I looked in my purse, some of my cigarettes were gone!

I: Thank you, Miss Simpson. That's all for now.

Contents of Vita Simpson's purse. Clockwise from top left: lipstick, cold cream, keys to her flat and automobile, facial tissues, lighter, wallet containing just over five pounds, powder compact, perfume bottle (sample taken confirmed to be perfume), address book which had information for Ambrose Belvoir, Mabel Hickney, Felix Darlington, Roy Peterson, and Lord Chomley.

Undated photograph of Alfred, Lord Chomley, at his country house, Wuthers

Police photograph of Alfred, Lord Chomley, taken at 19 Tootley Row, 28 November 1933, 12:22 A.M.

Fragments of a poison pen letter believed to belong to Lord Chomley, found in the fireplace

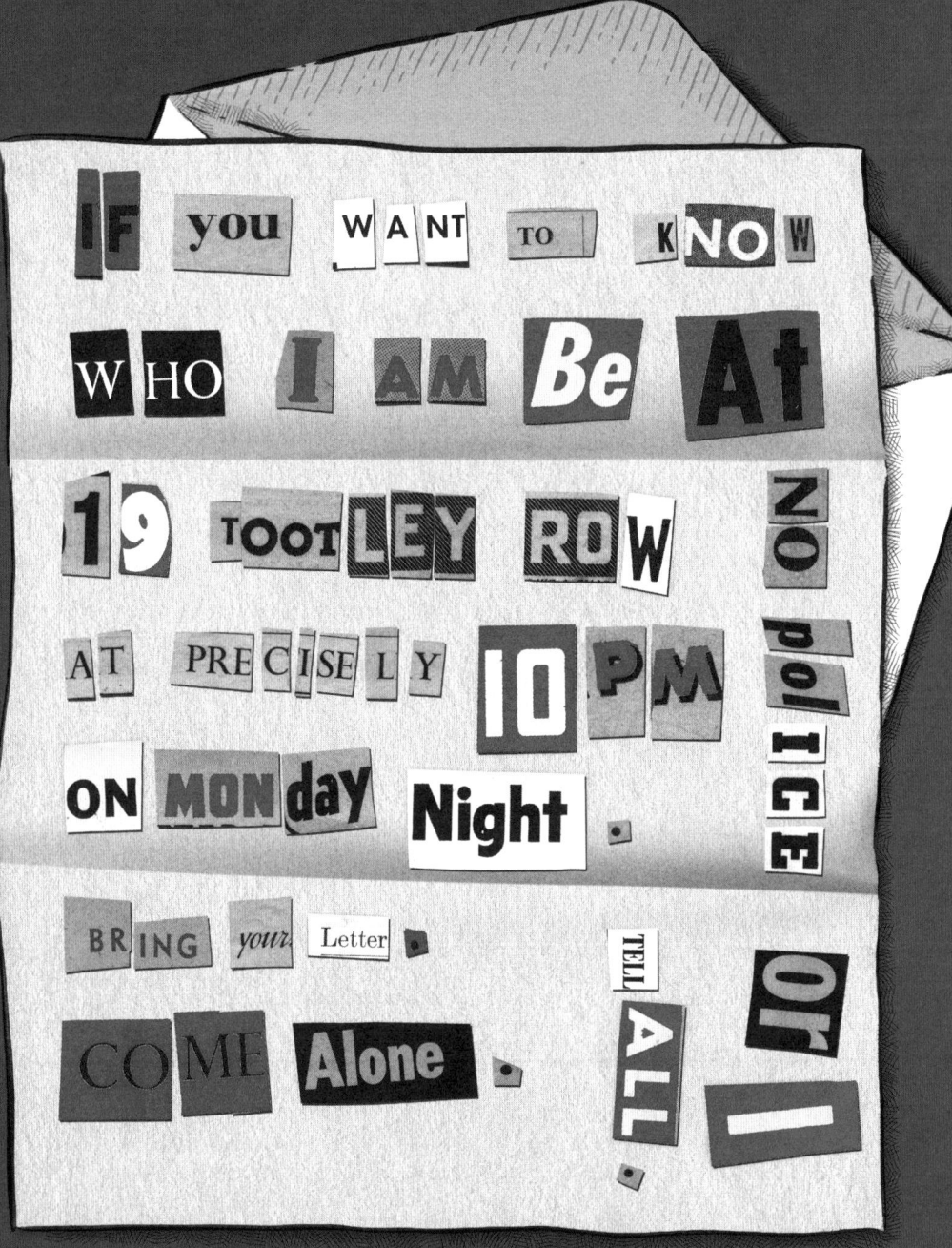

Letter received by Lord Chomley on Sunday, 26 November 1933

INTERVIEW WITH LORD ALFRED CHOMLEY

28 November, 1:25–1:35 A.M.

LC: Do sit down, dear boy.

I: Yes, sir. I was about to.

LC: Good, good. No need to stand in my presence. I'm great chums with the police. Lord Dimbles, the superintendent, is a friend of mine. You've handled this very well and I shall put in a good word for you. Ghastly business. I'm sure you'll do a smashing job working it out. Now, you can set up a time to come meet with me, as I'm sure you have all sorts of questions. My staff will get it top priority. I'm off shooting tomorrow, but . . .

I: We'll need to speak to you now, your lordship. Just a few questions.

LC: Well, I suppose I could do my part and answer a few questions.

I: Very good of you, sir. We understand that you received a letter, a poison pen letter.

LC: What? I know nothing of a poison pen letter. Came around tonight to see dear Ambrose. I wanted his advice on a bit of art I'm going to buy. A bust of Zeus by a daring young artist.

I: We know about your letter, sir. The constable pulled it from the fire.

LC: I'm sure I don't know. . . .

I: We will be most discreet, sir. But we do know you received a poison pen letter and a note telling you to come here tonight at an appointed time, just like everyone else.

LC: Well. Well. Of course. I can see you're a good chap. Discretion. Yes. I put high value on that sort of thing. Yes, I received some nonsense in the post and then a note telling me to come here. Assumed it was a bit of a wheeze by dear Ambrose. He's always up to something amusing.

I: When did you get your poison pen letter?

LC: About a week ago.

I: We can only make out a few words. There seems to be the word *dungeon*, and perhaps, down here, something about a pond?

LC: You know, I can't remember exactly.

I: No?

LC: I barely glanced at it. But it *was* something about a dungeon. Wuthers was constructed in the mid-eighteenth century on the site of a much older house that had a dungeon in the basement. The dungeon was kept when they built the new house. We use it to store wine.

I: And the pond?

LC: No idea, I'm afraid. Actually, no, now that I think of it. It wasn't pond—it was ponga. Which is a silver fern native to New Zealand. That's right. I'm a bit of a naturalist, you see. I love my gardens. I have plants from all over the world. Yes, this was about my ponga.

I: So the note was about your dungeon and your silver fern?

LC: Something like that.

I: I see, sir. And when did the second note arrive, the one telling you to come here tonight?

LC: Sunday morning. My man brought it in to me while I was having my bath. Seemed a bit of nonsense, but as I said, Ambrose is always good for a laugh, so I thought I'd pop round. I had been planning to go to a dinner for the Friends of the British Museum. I'm sponsoring a bit of a dig in Mesopotamia. But I thought I'd come by here on the way, and, of course, the evening took a turn.

I: Must have been quite a late dinner, sir.

LC: Oh yes. No good dinner starts before ten. Missing it now, of course, because of this.

I: Very sorry, sir.

LC: Can't be helped, can't be helped. So I came round, and there was Ambrose answering his own door! Extraordinary. And there everyone was—dear Vita, Felix, Peterson, Mabel, and someone who looked vaguely familiar that I'm told was my former cook. Extraordinary!

I: Indeed. So the group was assembled when you arrived.

LC: Yes.

I: And Roy Peterson was in the chair by the fire.

LC: Dead asleep, yes . . . oh. That's rather awkward, isn't it, with the fellow being actually dead. Deeply asleep. A not uncommon condition for Peterson. The man likes a drink. No sooner had I arrived and asked what was going on than in came a constable with tales of murder.

I: Which is when you put your note in the fire?

LC: Must have dropped it in surprise.

I: Of course, sir. Did you go near Mr. Peterson at all?

LC: Only to have a look at him, as the constable said he was dead. Told me to stand back. I don't hold it against him. Only doing his duty.

I: Did anyone approach Mr. Peterson before that?

LC: Not at all. But again, I was the last to arrive. I have no idea what went on before my arrival.

I: I see. Now, sir, something has come up related to you. A man named Desmond Plott. He was one of your footmen. He died at Wuthers on New Year's Eve.

LC: Plott! Yes, of course. Terrible thing. I had a marvelous party that night, and at breakfast the next morning I'm told there's a dead footman in one of the ponds! Naturally, I said to get him out. Terrible thing for a guest to see. And luckily one of the guests, dear friend of mine, doctor from Harley Street, was there. Went out and had a look. Said he drowned. Clearly drunk.

I: Did you call the local police?

LC: I went right to the top, of course! Everything was done perfectly, and we had the poor boy taken off and treated with the utmost care. I paid for the funeral. Felt I had to. Owed it to the boy.

I: Why was that?

LC: That is how the lord of the manor should act.

I: Do you know how he drowned?

LC: Got drunk at the party, apparently. Was taking a bit too much of the champagne. I can't begrudge the boy. Must have wandered out, quite blotto. It was a filthy December night, terrible fog. Must have stumbled right into the pond, poor bugger. Now, I think that's about all the time . . .

I: I have one more question, your lordship. We found this and thought it might belong to you.

```
Lord Chomley was shown the pill
case, closed.
```

LC: Never seen it before.

I: It looks similar to your lighter and cigarette case.

LC: It does indeed. That's fashion for you, my boy. Simple good taste. No. Never seen it. Now, I must be going. Do give my regards to the superintendent. I'll see him next month.

Contents of Lord Chomley's pockets. Clockwise from top left: lighter, cigarette case, wallet.

NOTES

All interviews at the house were complete and all suspects were released at two in the morning. Ambrose Belvoir and George Baxter had to leave 19 Tootley Row; Lord Chomley invited them both to stay at his London house, where he was currently in residence. The first and most natural thought, given the nature of the gathering, is that Roy Peterson was murdered by one or more members of the group and the rest kept silent because of the letters. What cannot be explained by this theory is the fact that we were alerted to come to the scene of what was obviously a premeditated act.

19 TOOTLEY ROW

We sealed 19 Tootley Row for two days before allowing them to return. We found no additional clues during this time—and I can assure you, we took that sitting room apart looking for devices, hidden panels, traps, anything at all. We found nothing but an ordinary sitting room and an ordinary chair. We combed through the remains of the fire and found nothing more than a fragment of newspaper and a cigarette butt along with the charred logs. The bottles in the bar and the glasses contained only normal alcohol. While we did find cocaine in Mr. Belvoir's upstairs room, we found no morphine.

THE LETTERS

The paper type, envelopes, glue, and source materials are all quite ordinary. The newspapers and magazines used to create them are readily available in London. The only piece of physical evidence of note on or about the letters was the hair stuck to the gum seal of the tailor's letter. The hair trapped in the gum seal of the tailor's letter was brown, 3.5 inches in length. The color and length most closely matched Mabel Hickney's.

OTHER WITNESSES

We made door-to-door inquiries to see if anyone had witnessed anything of note. Miss Henrietta Doome of 22 Tootley Row is a keen observer of the neighborhood. She invited the constables in for tea and biscuits and retrieved a notebook in which she kept her "little notes" about what happened on the street.

Miss Doome had witnessed, on twenty-three recorded occasions over many months, a man—not known to be Ambrose Belvoir or George Baxter—coming and going from 19 Tootley Row. This man was always seen to take the stairs down to the lower entrance. After the first few times she observed the man, Miss Doome watched 19 Tootley Row through a pair of opera glasses and saw the man opening the kitchen window, reaching inside, removing a box, and then opening the door. This was always after ten in the evening. Many observations were made in the summer, when the days are long. She reported that it was harder to see exactly what the man was doing on the dark winter nights, but she had certainly observed him in the area. She was not observing 19 Tootley Row on the night of the murder, as she was staying with her sister in Reading.

This information triggered a thought. I went back through the photographs we took at the scene. Our photographer went back and forth between taking photos of the rooms and the suspects. He took the initial photograph of the kitchen window at 12:15, came upstairs to take photographs of the suspects, and returned downstairs to finish taking photos. The next kitchen photo was taken at 12:25. There is a box next to the window at 12:15 that is not there at 12:25.

We brought Mr. George Baxter in to Scotland Yard for a second interview.

SECOND INTERVIEW WITH GEORGE BAXTER, CONDUCTED AT THE YARD

28 November 1933, 3:00 p.m.

I: Thank you for coming in, Mr. Baxter.

GB: Of course. Yes. Of course.

I: We just have a few more questions about the events at 19 Tootley Row.

GB: Anything to help, of course. I wasn't there, though. As you know. When it happened.

I: Yes, we've established you were elsewhere at the time of the murder. However, I think you may have misled us in some of your answers. You have a neighbor who regularly sees a man come down the steps to the kitchen entrance late in the evening. He opens the window, reaches inside, and then opens the kitchen door. This same neighbor has seen the man leave either later in the night or early in the morning.

GB: Oh, that nosey cow. The one always peering out with her opera glasses. She's just a gossip, inspector. Pay no mind to her.

I: That's as may be, Mr. Baxter, but we noticed something in the photographs we took at the scene. There is a photograph of the kitchen window taken at 12:15 that shows a small box to the right of the window. The photographer went upstairs at that time to take photographs of those present at the party and you were permitted to remove a change of clothes from your room downstairs. You had a constable with you, but it seems he was distracted, because when the next photo of the kitchen was taken at 12:25, the box by the window was gone. Because you removed it.

GB: Oh, I'm sure . . . I . . .

I: I suspect that you keep a key in that box, Mr. Baxter. Why did you remove it? There's no point in lying to us.

GB: Will this get back to Mr. Belvoir, sir?

I: Never mind that! This is a murder inquiry.

GB: Yes, sir. Of course, sir. I just didn't think it was relevant, sir . . .

I: You leave it to us to decide what's relevant. Tell me about the key.

GB: I have a friend who visits, inspector. It's simply for him to come inside.

I: Who is this friend?

GB: His name is Phillip Barrett. He's a valet as well and we have a drink or a cigarette at the end of the day sometimes. He has nothing to do with this, and neither do I! When I took the box, the key was there, just as it should have been.

I: Is Mr. Belvoir aware of this key or your visitor?

GB: I'm not sure, sir. I don't think so. But . . .

I: But?

GB: If there were parties going on upstairs, Phillip would sometimes slip up there and get a cocktail. I believe he encountered Mr. Belvoir on at least one of these occasions, but Mr. Belvoir thought he was an invited guest and thought nothing of it. Mr. Belvoir is generous and liberal in his hospitality. But I tell you, Phillip and I were at the Green Cat. Everything else I said was true! And, I have something!

Mr. Baxter produced a photograph from his pocket. It showed Mr. Belvoir in the hallway of the house, wearing his red dressing gown.

GB: Earlier in the evening, Mr. Belvoir was trying on a dressing gown he had received as a gift. He asked me to take a photograph of him wearing it to send to the person who gave it to him. I have the photo.

I: You took this yesterday and have it already?

GB: A friend of mine is a photographer. He developed it for me. It shows I was there at five o'clock.

I: We know you were there at five o'clock, Mr. Baxter. This doesn't explain why you didn't tell us there was a key, or a regular visitor, or why you took the box.

GB: But it's something, isn't it? I was there, doing my duties, exactly as I said.

I: What other photographs do you have?

GB: This was the last one of the roll of film. The others were of my friends, just personal ones. I used the last one for Mr. Belvoir. And yes, later that night I took away the box by the window because I knew Phillip's fingerprints would be all over it, and that there was a key in it. I have a visitor, inspector. That's all. I know nothing of this murder. Phillip certainly knows nothing of this murder.

I: Is there anything else you haven't told us?

GB: No, sir. Well, I did notice one thing—when I went to get my change of clothes, I noticed a pair of Mr. Belvoir's shoes in my wardrobe. I am certain they were not there earlier. And I am certain they are Mr. Belvoir's. They'd gone missing months ago. Mr. Belvoir thought he must have lost them during a spirited evening. How they ended up in my wardrobe that night, I have no idea. But I didn't want to mention it because I was so worried about the key.

I: Is that everything, now?

GB: Yes, sir! Everything!

We fully investigated Phillip Barrett. On the evening in question, he was witnessed along with Mr. Baxter at the Green Cat. At no point did either leave the restaurant, and neither left the sight of other members of the party for more than a few minutes, and only to go to the toilet, which is located at the back of the restaurant and has no window or outside door. They left together at 11:30 p.m. Mr. Barrett returned to his place of employment, and Mr. Baxter returned to 19 Tootley Row. While this eliminates Mr. Baxter and Mr. Barrett, it introduces the fact that there was another key to the house, and that that key was kept in an easily accessible place by the broken window. This suggests that someone could have gained entry to the house by breaking the pane, unlocking and opening the window, and taking the key.

Photograph of Ambrose Belvoir, taken by George Baxter at 5 P.M. on 27 November 1933

Undated photograph of Edward Finsdale, tailor, at his shop

INTERVIEW WITH EDWARD FINSDALE, TAILOR, CONDUCTED AT HIS SHOP

28 November 1933, 9 A.M.

I: Could you tell me what happened last evening?

EF: Of course, sir. My shop closes for business every evening at five P.M. I then walk home to have dinner with my wife. That evening she had prepared a most delicious roast with an egg custard to finish. I read a book by the fire—I have been rereading my Trollope and have reached *The Eustace Diamonds*—and took a half-hour rest. Then I returned to my shop as I do every weekday evening from eight until ten-thirty. I often bring my dog, Fergus, with me. He is a Scottish terrier. He dislikes the rain, so I did not bring him along on that occasion. It was a nasty evening, sir. Nasty. But of course I have a Brigg umbrella.

I: Yes, sir. And you arrived at eight?

EF: Five minutes after eight. I was walking slowly due to the rain and wind. I unlocked the shop and set my umbrella in the stand. Of course, I looked at the floor to make sure I hadn't tracked messy footprints into the shop. There was no letter there at the time. I made my way back to my workroom, switched on the wireless, made a cup of tea, and finished a suit I was to have ready for one of my gentlemen in the morning. I was most eager to complete it. I was finished by ten-fifteen, so I tidied up for fifteen minutes before putting on my coat in preparation for leaving. It was then I found the note on the floor by the door—this strange piece of paper telling me to call the police because there had been a murder. I didn't know what to make of it. At first, I thought it must be some sort of distasteful joke. I was going to put it right in the bin, but something about the letter concerned me. I fretted for some moments, sir, before I finally picked up the telephone and called the police.

I: You were quite right to do so.

EF: Oh, thank you for saying so, sir. It was most extraordinary. The constable came and was exceedingly polite. A credit to the force, sir. He put my mind at rest and took the note away. I would have thought no more of it, but then, of course, I read the terrible news this morning. I couldn't eat my breakfast, sir, and my wife had prepared an excellent plate of kippers. I ended up giving them to Fergus, who was most appreciative.

I: Do you know Ambrose Belvoir?

EF: I am not acquainted with Mr. Belvoir personally. I have seen his photograph in the papers. I suspect his tailor may be French, or at one of the newer establishments in Soho. His suits are not the sort of thing I make for my gentlemen.

I: Do you know any of the persons involved in the case?

```
Note: I then presented Mr. Finsdale
with a list of those present at
19 Tootley Row that evening.
```

EF: I do not. I am at a loss, sir, as to why this note was left with me.

I: Your habits, Mr. Finsdale, they are regular?

EF: *Most* regular, sir. A good tailor is precise in his habits. Some measure twice and cut once. I measure thrice.

I: It seems whoever left the note knew your habits, when you came in and out of your shop in the evening. It seems that your regularity may have been the reason you were chosen.

EF: This is most dreadful. But you know, inspector, Fergus has been vigilant lately. When I bring him to the shop in the evening, he spends most of the time sleeping in his basket by the electric fire. But for the last—let me think—week or so, I suppose, he's kept a watch on the front door like a little soldier. I thought he was watching other dogs go by. He yipped quite a few times in the evenings, now that I think of it, and one time he even growled, and Fergus is not a growler, inspector. He is a most polite little man. He must have sensed something was wrong! Oh dear. Oh dear. I've lost my appetite again, and I believe my wife has gotten some excellent kidneys for a pie. Oh *dear!* I suppose Fergus will be having my portion.

Fergus the Scottish terrier, whom I met at this conclusion of this interview and who seemed to be a most sensible dog. I trust dogs more than I trust people. Dogs do not lie. I believe Fergus saw someone observing the shop and did his best to inform his owner, and it seems entirely appropriate that he should be rewarded with kidney pie for his efforts.

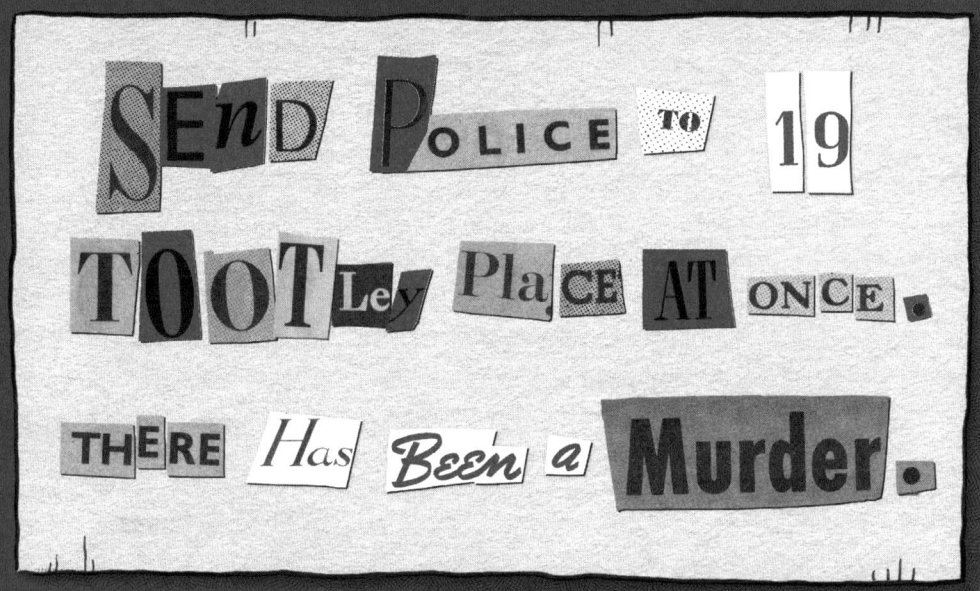

Letter left under door of Finsdale's Fine Tailoring on 27 November 1933, sometime after 8:05 P.M.

Undated photograph of Gibbons Restaurant

INTERVIEW WITH BERNARD WELLS, HEADWAITER AT GIBBONS, CONDUCTED AT RESTAURANT

28 November 1933, 10 A.M.

I: I was hoping you could tell me everything that happened from the time Mr. Peterson entered the restaurant on Monday night until the time he left. Nothing is insignificant.

BW: I will endeavor to do my best, sir.

I: Mr. Peterson was a regular patron?

BW: Oh yes, sir. Every night, or quite nearly. Certainly five or more times a week. Always alone.

I: What time did he arrive?

BW: He was earlier than normal on Monday night. He usually appears after nine.

I: What time did he arrive last night?

BW: Ten minutes to eight. I had a fright when I saw him, sir, because I thought I must be off on my time and checked the clock. And then, he requested a table by the window. That was unusual. He normally prefers the back, away from the door. Mr. Peterson doesn't like the cold breeze from the door. Or . . . the other people. He is a private man. This is unfortunate for him, inspector. We are known for being a place to see and be seen.

I: And did you seat him by the window?

BW: Yes, sir. We arranged a table for one for him immediately.

I: He was alone?

BW: Mr. Peterson always dines alone and reads or writes in a notebook while he eats. I think he enjoys our quiet atmosphere. And our American cocktails. He enjoys a corpse reviver.

I: I beg your pardon?

BW: Oh dear. That's unfortunate. That's the name of his preferred cocktail—the corpse reviver number two. The name comes from the fact that it is quite potent, in flavor and in alcoholic content—strong enough to raise the dead, you see? It's comprised of Kina Lillet, Cointreau, gin, and absinthe.

I: So he had one of those . . .

BW: He had five, sir.

I: Witnesses did say he appeared rather intoxicated, so that explains that.

BW: That's a regular number for Mr. Peterson. He has a prodigious tolerance.

I: Did he order dinner?

BW: Yes, sir. He had the lamb stew. And he wasn't reading a book or writing. He seemed preoccupied, mostly looking out the window. He pulled a sheet of paper from his pocket several times, read it, and returned it his pocket. He spent much of the night looking out the window, watching the street. A man came inside to speak to him, which resulted in some unpleasantness.

I: Did you recognize this man?

BW: No, sir. I think he was just passing and happened to have a copy of Mr. Peterson's novel—*Hendrickson's Bag* or something like that? Forgive me, sir. I've seen it in all the shops but I've never read it.

I: Neither have I. That's quite all right.

BW: Well, this man had a copy in his shopping bag and must have seen Mr. Peterson in the window and was delighted. He came inside to ask for an autograph. Mr. Peterson was quite vocal in his displeasure. The man ran off in terror. Another party asked to be moved farther away from Mr. Peterson's table.

I: What did the man look like?

BW: I couldn't say, sir. Just a man in a black coat and a black hat. Clean-shaven, I think. Maybe a thin moustache. I was very busy at that moment. We had an issue with our fishmonger and ran out of haddock and crab early in the evening. That caused some fuss. A patron dropped a napkin down the toilet, so we had a bit of a flood that I had to distract from while it was fixed and tidied. So our toilet was out of service for a short while. And we had some of our more prominent guests in. Many of our customers are in the arts or on the stage. We had Lily Morgan, the actress, in with Donald Gremby, the director. Morgana Frood, the sculptress, was here. All three came in while Mr. Peterson was here.

I: Did they interact with Mr. Peterson?

BW: No. A nod, perhaps. That was all. Regular guests know it's best not to approach him. Especially how he looked that night, sir. His expression was quite grim.

I: What time did he leave?

BW: I think it was around nine, sir. I couldn't be exactly sure. I know he normally has pudding, but he didn't on Monday, and he didn't finish his meal either. He left a large gratuity because he didn't wait for his change, and that wasn't like him at all. I don't like to speak ill of our guests, or the dead, but . . . he wasn't a nice man. But a customer is still a customer.

Undated photograph of Bernard Wells, headwaiter at Gibbons Restaurant

SECOND INTERVIEW WITH AMBROSE BELVOIR, CONDUCTED AT SCOTLAND YARD

29 November 1933, noon

I: Please have a seat, Mr. Belvoir. Thank you for coming.

AB: Of course. Happy to be of service.

I: Mr. Belvoir, are you aware that your valet, Mr. Baxter, has been keeping a spare key to your house in a box by the kitchen window—and that this key is used by a friend of Mr. Baxter to gain admittance to your house for social calls?

AB: Does he! How scandalous.

I: Did you have any knowledge of this key?

AB: None at all.

I: What about a man named Phillip Barrett?

AB: No. Unless he is one of the Bristol Barretts?

I: I don't believe he is.

AB: Then no. Is this the person who comes in for the social calls?

I: Yes.

AB: Remarkable.

I: Do you consider this to be a dismissible offense, having guests take a secret key to come in at night?

AB: I'd dismiss him if he didn't, inspector. This is what you must understand about my house—it is open, as am I. An open book. But this gives me a theory, inspector. Would you like to hear it?

I: Please.

AB: What if an enterprising burglar, seeing George go out for the evening, had a bit of a brainstorm. He knew about the key and decided that the downstairs would be unsupervised and he should come in and have a little look around. Meanwhile, Roy arrived at the house and needed to powder his nose. What if he went to the downstairs loo because he wanted something from the kitchen as well and surprised said burglar. He tried to fight the burglar off and ended up getting stabbed in the process. The naughty chap runs off. Locks the door and puts the key back as a way of making it seem like the deed must have been done by someone inside the house. Roy, who I've heard was up to the gills with morphine, took the fatal instrument and came back upstairs, injured. We were none the wiser. He sat down, dropped the ice pick on the floor, and tragically died in front of us.

I: That's very interesting, Mr. Belvoir.

AB: Thank you. As a young boy, I loved a Sherlock Holmes or two for breakfast. It's just the only thing I can think of that conforms to all the facts.

I: Was anything missing from the downstairs?

AB: Clearly, someone took my ice pick, but that was found, unfortunately.

I: Why do you think Mr. Peterson might have been so full of morphine?

AB: Nerves, inspector. The letter had him on edge. Roy could put away a drink. Perhaps he needed something stronger.

I: I'll bear that in mind as we continue our investigation.

AB: It's just . . . well, nothing else makes any sense, does it? Unless it was one of those "stabbed with an ice pick made of ice" kinds of mysteries. Oh, that would be something. An ice pick made of ice that was of the exact same measurements as my ice pick. That's something to think about!

I: We'll be sure to consider that as well. A question, though, in the open-book spirit . . .

AB: Fire away!

I: Did you like Mr. Peterson?

AB: I think *like* is the wrong word. He was a personality, and I like personalities.

I: What about the others? Did they like him?

AB: Well, I can't speak for them, of course. I don't know the Adder woman. Chomley is a collector of personalities as well, for different reasons. I think he enjoyed having Peterson around. I don't pretend to know what Mabel thinks about anything. Vita found him to be quite sweet because he had so many cats. I'm not sure Felix pays attention to other men. I think he sees a kind of shape in the cigarette smoke where they're standing next to an attractive woman, and that's about it.

I: And the matter of Desmond Plott? His death after the New Year's Eve party at Wuthers? Might you have any other thoughts on that matter, since you're here?

AB: You know, inspector, I've racked my brain for the last day about that—about all of this. I recall so little of that night. Felix was in a foul mood, that I remember. My friend Morgana said she found me having a spirited debate with a potted palm, and I have a vague recollection of trying to exit the house through the piano.

I: Any recollections of Desmond Plott?

AB: That he existed. The champagne didn't come from thin air. Someone had to pour it. I'm afraid that's all I have. He worked for Chomley.

I: And what kind of a man is Lord Chomley?

AB: A very interesting one indeed, inspector. Loves the sea. Has a bit of a fascination with mollusks.

I: Do you know anything about a dungeon at Wuthers?

AB: Goodness, no, but it must be a rather wonderful place. I will ask to see it sometime.

I: Well, thank you for coming in and talking to us about the key.

AB: While I'm here, George told me he took a rather dashing photograph of me in my new dressing gown. He said he's given it to you. May I see it?

```
I removed the photograph from
the files and presented it to
Mr. Belvoir.
```

AB: Oh, heavens, that does look good. The dressing gown is a gift from a friend in Morocco. Magnificent garment. Could I have this, inspector? We took it to send to her. I'm not sure what value it has to you, but my friend would love it.

I: You can have it back when we've concluded our investigation.

AB: Very kind. When you find the right light, it's a bit of a gift from above, you know? I do look rather marvelous!

Following any notable case, we always receive anonymous letters, most of which are written by cranks. However, not all anonymous letters can be dismissed. On the second of December, the following letter was received at Scotland Yard, addressed to me. It could not be traced.

> I saw what happened to that author fellow and that he was at Gibbons Restaurant on the night he was murdered. Something has been eating at me and I have to tell you in case it helps you find the person who did it.
>
> I work in a shop near Gibbons and someone left an envelope on the counter for me with a pound in it and told me to go there on the night of the 27th and have dinner using the money. The only thing I had to do was take the dinner napkin to the loo and flush it down the toilet at 8:30. The note said if I did this I'd get another envelope with a pound in it for my trouble. Honest I thought a plumber did it for the work or something and that's a lot of money and free dinner at Gibbons which is quite nice so I did it. I saw the author fellow and he seemed very unpleasant but that is not a reason to kill someone.
>
> I was upset when I read about the murder and I knew I had seen him there so I burned the note. But I can't sleep for worry and guilt. I just wanted you to know and I am sorry if I had something to do with it. I can't see how I could have because all I did was put a napkin in a toilet. It is just very strange. Also I never got the other pound.

Bernard Wells, the headwaiter at Gibbons Restaurant, could not recall any specifics about a new customer who paid with a one-pound note that night, but this is not surprising given how many people dine at Gibbons and pay with pound notes.

LETTER CONTENT

We must now get into the content of the letters.

FELIX DARLINGTON

Felix Darlington confessed to hitting a man with his car. We were able to find the record of this accident. It took place on 2 April 1933. The victim was Peter Dudley, age fifty-one, a local eccentric who was known to collect squirrels to raise as pets. (Upon his death, seventy-four squirrels were found inside his house.) He had a habit of wandering into the road in front of cars while chasing after a desired squirrel. He was noted to be intensely focused on the task, and had been previously hit by a bicycle. Because of this, and because Mr. Darlington reported the accident, no charge was filed.

AMBROSE BELVOIR, VITA SIMPSON, AND MABEL HICKNEY

Ambrose Belvoir, Vita Simpson, and Mabel Hickney received letters concerning the death of Billie Snooks—and, generally, there was a grain of truth in those letters.

    The death of Billie Snooks was the subject of feverish media coverage. Billie Snooks was a twenty-five-year-old actress. She had gained fame in productions such as: *Six Jolly Fellows, All Aboard!, On a Moonless Night*, and *Seven Sailors and Sister Sally*. She had just filmed her first motion picture, *The Lady with the Glass Arrow,* a month before her death on 11 February 1933. She was found dead in her bed by Mabel Hickney, who lived in the flat with her. The cause of death was an overdose. All indications suggested that the overdose was accidental. That has never been challenged.

    Miss Snooks's lifestyle was brutally examined by the press as well. At first, she was treated with sympathy, but then she was painted as a person living a wanton life of socializing, sex, and drug use. She was romantically linked to several famous men. It should be noted that many of these details were provided by Mabel Hickney.

ACTRESS FOUND DEAD OF DRUG OVERDOSE

POPULAR WEST END ACTRESS AND FILM STAR BILLIE SNOOKS DIES AFTER NIGHT OF DANCING AND DRUGS

Popular West End actress Billie Snooks was found dead in her bed this morning, following an evening of dancing, drinking, and drugs. Earlier in the evening, Miss Snooks was onstage in her current play, *Golden Whispers*. She then went to Lady Jesper's Never-Never Ball in Mayfair. Miss Snooks was photographed wearing a daring, almost translucent dress designed by Norris LaRue. During the ball, Miss Snooks is said to have consumed large amounts of cocaine. After a champagne breakfast at dawn, she returned to her flat in Mayfair with her sister, Mabel Hickney, who also resides there. When Snooks had not appeared by late the next afternoon, Miss Hickney entered her bedroom and found her dead, an assortment of drugs on the table next to her bed.

Spent Last Night of Her Life in Daring Gown

Actress's Sister Tells of Terrible Discovery

"OH, SHE WAS DEAD!"

DESCRIBES TABLE FULL OF DRUGS

Mabel Hickney, sister of the late Billie Snooks, tells of the horrible scene at Craven Mansions. Miss Mabel Hickney shared the flat with her famous sister and attended Lady Jesper's Never-Never Ball with her the evening before. "I woke early, as I always do, and began my day, I did some shopping and had lunch with a friend. When I came back to the flat in the evening, I could see Billie still hadn't emerged from her bedroom, so I went in to offer her a cup of tea. And . . . oh! I could see something was wrong! She was a terrible color and not moving. I tried to rouse her, but I could see she was . . . oh, she was dead! I called for help and the police came. I knew, of course, what had done it. She took drugs, you see. Terrible drugs. I told her she had to stop. I know the police found a lacquered box containing cocaine on the table next to her bed, as well as two vials of morphine and sleeping tablets."

SISTER REVEALS SHOCKING DETAILS OF STARLET'S TRAGIC DEATH

"It's easier to get cocaine than a cup of tea!"

Tells of men coming to her sister's flat at all hours

"It was cocaine! So much cocaine!" said Miss Hickney, speaking of her sister's death. "The evil, terrible stuff! She would go mad on it, running and dancing around the room. I begged her to stop because I knew she was going to die if she kept on like this. Oh, the cocaine! You can get it anywhere at those parties. They pass it around in little boxes. It's easier to get cocaine than a cup of tea! Men would come around day and night—all sorts of society types. They'd disappear into her room. I saw so many men. Famous ones, as well."

THE DESMOND PLOTT CONNECTIONS

ROY PETERSON

We now come to the matter of Desmond Plott and the events of 31 December 1932. Roy Peterson's letter directly implicates him in some way in the death of Desmond Plott and suggests there was a witness. (As does the crumpled note in his pocket.)

LORD CHOMLEY

Obviously, we did not believe the "pon" in Lord Chomley's letter referred to his silver fern. That letter was about Desmond Plott and his death in the pond at Wuthers. What it said exactly, we do not know. It does make reference to a dungeon.

CLORIS ADDER

Cloris Adder's letter contains the least serious accusation of the group. Why was she included? The connection seems to be that she was at Wuthers on 31 December 1932, and would likely have known Desmond Plott better than anyone else present.

I made inquiries about Desmond Plott's death to the local police and found that there was very little information. His death was recorded as an accidental drowning due to intoxication. The cause of death was determined by a Dr. Fergus Anderson, who was a party guest. The body was immediately sent to Plott's family in London for burial. There was no postmortem examination, and, as it was found to be an accident, no photographs were taken of the body or scene. I found the overall record of the event to be very thin and sensed hesitation in the voice of the chief constable of the area when discussing the matter.

I made plans to send someone up to Gloucester to make quiet inquiries, but we had an unfortunate incident at our annual pre-holiday police dinner. One of the dishes—a crab-and-mayonnaise salad—proved to be spoiled, and over thirty officers were badly sickened. I had no one to spare.

My sister's boy, Nigel Stickley, has been keen on policing for some time and wants to be a detective. Lacking a better option, I sent him with instructions to talk to some locals and find out what he could about what happened at Wuthers on New Year's Eve. It was better than doing nothing, which was the only other option. He took the train to Mumbles-on-Poot, the closest town to Wuthers. I have attached his reports. Please do note that I truly had no other options available to me at the time. I allowed him the title of special constable, which he seems to have taken quite seriously.

THE FROG & BUCKET

MUMBLES-ON-POOT, GLOUCESTERSHIRE

```
Telephone:
Don't think they have one

6 December 1933
```

Dear Uncle Detective Chief Inspector Harold Jensen,

It's your nephew Nigel Stickley reporting in from Mumbles-on-Poot. I arrived last evening and have taken a room above the local pub, The Frog & Bucket. The room is nice but the bed squeaks quite loudly. I am a light sleeper, as I am sure Mum has told you, but I will try not to let it affect me as I will have to get used to this sort of thing when I am on The Force.

After unpacking and having a cheese sandwich that Mum packed for me (she packed me enough sandwiches for two days along with plenty of biscuits), I prepared myself. I have packed several Disguises. I put on the one I call "rustic country fellow" (I have decided to call him Will Crabbe in honor of the crab salad that got me here).

I set out walking toward Wuthers. It is within three miles of town and was a very nice walk. I thought how quick the trip would have been on my bicycle, but that was back in London. I practiced being Will Crabbe as I went, slowing my walk and making rustic greetings to anyone who passed. I think I did very well!

Wuthers is surrounded by a stone wall with an imposing gate. I considered going over the wall, but found it was easier to climb the gate, even though I tore my trousers a bit doing so. Once over, I found I was in a massive garden—more like a park! There was almost no one in sight, so I was able to walk around and have a look. I found a rake as I went, so I used it as part of my Disguise. I have drawn you a map of the grounds. I also brought my new camera and took some photographs. You will see that there are many interesting statues on the grounds.

I was taking a photo of myself on the grounds using my self-timer when the head gardener found me and expelled me from the property rather forcefully. I will continue my work here in town and find as much information as I can.

Yours truly,

Special Constable Nigel Stickley
Your Nephew

WOODS

SOME MAD GARDEN THAT GOES IN CIRCLES, GOT LOST IN HERE FOR **4** HOURS

BEES! (GOT STUNG **3** TIMES!)

HOUSE, VERY BIG

MORE WOODS

DOGS

HORSES

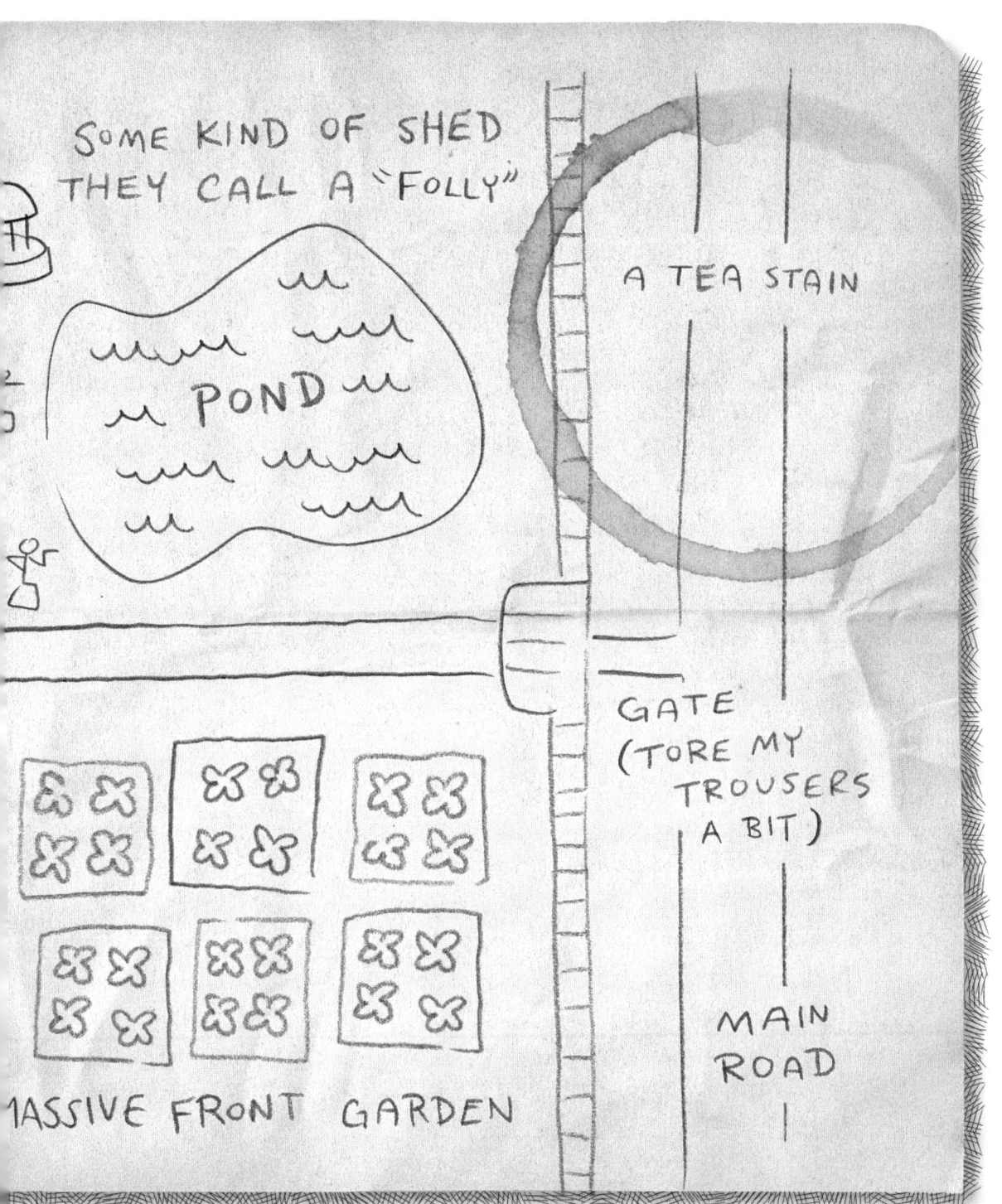

Map of Wuthers, as drawn by Nigel Stickley

**Photographs of Wuthers taken by
Nigel Stickley on 6 December 1933**

THE FROG & BUCKET

MUMBLES-ON-POOT, GLOUCESTERSHIRE

Telephone:
I checked they do not have one

7 December 1933

Dear Uncle Detective Chief Inspector Harold Jensen,

There's been a development since the letter I mailed yesterday! I was in the pub downstairs in my new Disguise, "Edward Plank," a tourist. I used my self-timer to take a photograph of myself enjoying a pint, as a tourist might. The man next to me asked if I was a reporter! I said no. He asked me if I was sure, because if I was, he had something I might be interested in, something about what went on at Wuthers.

Of course I immediately told him I was part of The Force and that he was bound to tell me what he knew. He didn't seem to believe that I was a police officer and after a while, I was going to have him call you at Scotland Yard to prove it. Then he said, "I have information about what happened at Wuthers."

We went up to my room to speak in private and I wrote down what happened next. You will remember I took that course in Gregg shorthand so that I would be able to record conversations quickly.

ME: So, who are you?

MAN: I work at Wuthers. I'm a footman. Not for long. After this, I'm off. I've got a new job in London. I've had it with this place.

ME: What is your name?

MAN: You don't need my name.

ME: Well, what should I call you? I can't just call you man.

MAN: Call me Bob, then, if you like. It's not my real name.

ME: A code name!

BOB: Whatever you like.

ME: All right, Bob. What can you tell me about what happened at Wuthers on New Year's Eve?

BOB: Well, first I can tell you that his lordship is a dirty bird.

ME: What do you mean?

BOB: He has two kinds of parties, his lordship. First kind are the fancy ones, with the artsy London types. But then he has the other ones. Smaller ones. His special parties for his club. He calls it the Octopus Society. None of us are supposed to know about it, but he's got little octopus decorations everywhere, and also, we have eyes. Those are the parties where he and his friends go to the dungeon with the chains.

ME: Why?

BOB: Why do you think?

ME: Well, what are they doing down there with chains?

BOB: Think about it.

ME: I have a chain for my bicycle. But who rides a bicycle in a dungeon?

BOB: You aren't really with the police, are you?

ME: Yes, I am. So, what about these parties?

BOB: They have robes as well. Sometimes at night they come out on the lawn and drop the robes and dance around naked. We all sit and watch from the attic. Then you see them all at breakfast the next morning, all smiles like nothing had happened.

ME: Gosh!

BOB: Fair play to them, they can do as they like. It's just that, his lordship, he likes his secrets. Doesn't like people looking into his business. So when Desmond drowned, he was very upset, he was. I knew Desmond. Had a high opinion of himself, but I liked him. Didn't plan on being a footman long. He got on with everyone except Mrs. Adder, the cook. Nasty piece of work, that woman. Good food if she liked you, and if she didn't, she made sure you got the dregs. Always after Desmond. Always trying to get him into trouble with Spoonworth, the butler. Old Spoony we call him. Never worked, though, because his lordship liked Desmond. Anyway, this is how we get to the murder. You getting all of this?

ME: Yes. I took a course in Gregg shorthand for this very sort of thing.

BOB: Right. Well. Desmond fell for one of that fancy set—not an Octopus—an actress. He said she loved him too and he was going to leave Wuthers so they could be together.

ME: Who was it?

BOB: He never said her name. There were a number of actresses who came to Wuthers. I do know it was someone who was at that party, because something upset him that night. He said something about another man giving him trouble. He started drinking. We all drink a bit at those events, but he was drunk as a lord. Couldn't work. I think it was Adder who told old Spoony who chucked him out into the garden for the night and docked his pay. Last I saw Desmond, he was outside of the kitchen, smoking a cigarette. The next morning, one of the gardeners found him floating in the pond in the garden. Three of the gardeners brought him in, put him on the laundry floor. Old Spoony took over, pushed everyone out of the room. His lordship came down with a doctor friend of his named Anderson. The whole thing was over before noon. They took the body away. His lordship paid for the funeral and gave his family a bit of money and that was that.

ME: That's not a murder, though.

BOB: Thing is, you see, I saw Desmond when they brought him in. He had a gash in his head the size of an apple. He may have drowned, but someone caved his skull in first.

ME: Gosh!

BOB: Those that brought him in—they got very quiet and suddenly had a bit more money. Which is why I'm leaving. And you can have this and all...

Bob pulled two photographs from his pocket.

BOB: Here's Desmond. And here's a photograph from that night. All of them are in it—all the names I saw in the papers. Now, let's talk about my hundred pounds.

I wanted you to hear about all of that before I told you that I had to negotiate a price with him. We settled on the sum of £100, which is a lot of money, of course, but I knew you would want me to agree. I only had £5 on me, and I was using that to pay for my room at the inn. I gave him your name and telephone number to get the rest. You'll be hearing from him soon. I think he is on his way to the telephone box now so by the time you get this he's probably already reached you.

Yours truly,

Special Constable Nigel Stickley
Your Nephew

NOTE FROM HAROLD JENSEN: We quickly established that "Bob" is named David Finman and is indeed, or was, a footman at Wuthers. He has no criminal record and a straightforward history of employment. We found no reason to disbelieve what he had to say, even if he was taking payment for his story. The mention of Dr. Anderson and his timing of events matches our information and lends credence to his account. He left Wuthers immediately after speaking to Nigel and returned to London, where he took up work as a valet. (We paid the £100, but I will be docking it from Nigel's wages should he ever join the police.)

Undated photograph of Desmond Plott obtained by Nigel Stickley

Photo of Nigel Stickley as "Edward Plank" with "Bob" (David Finman) on the right

Photograph obtained by Nigel Stickley taken on 31 December 1932 at the New Year's Eve party at Wuthers

This photograph is profoundly interesting, as it captures all of the relevant parties in one image and was taken only a few hours before the death of Desmond Plott. Pictured from left to right: Roy Peterson, Mabel Hickney, Ambrose Belvoir, Desmond Plott, Cloris Adder, Vita Simpson, Lord Alfred Chomley, Billie Snooks, Felix Darlington.

This is where I leave the matter with you, Detective. I haven't a clue what to make of this. I feel that the answer is in here somewhere, but I just can't see it. May you have better luck with this than I have. I hope to hear from you soon.

Do you know who killed Roy Peterson? When you think you have solved the murder, read on for the solution.

Dear Detective,

When your letter arrived, it came as a relief. You are quite correct in your conclusions, of course. In thanks for your letter, here is one in return, containing all the details of the murder of Roy Peterson and the events that led to it.

We begin with Billie, beautiful Billie. Billie who sparkled and shone in whatever she was in. I only wish you had seen her perform. But perhaps you did? I hope so. We were cast together in *Lady Hercules*—she was the ingenue, I played her silly maid. I am a comic actress. (I truly appreciated your understanding of the art of performance. Playing the silly, unintelligent person is hard work. You must be impeccably aware of what it is you are not supposed to know, and, of course, timing is everything in comedy. You correctly saw how these facts came into play, and your generous words meant a great deal to me.)

We became the closest of friends. Sisters, really. I was a far better one than Mabel except in one way—along with Ambrose, I introduced Billie to cocaine. I was so naïve about the stuff. Everyone was using it. I tried it and found that it helped me keep up the pace—I could perform and dance all night. I could be witty and bright. Billie avoided it for a time, rightfully concerned that it could be dangerous. I said it was not. So, on my advice, she took it. She liked it far too much.

So many people fell in love with her. Felix Darlington was one. Billie had no interest in him, and that piqued his curiosity. Men always *desire* what they cannot have. Roy Peterson had also fallen in love with Billie. At first, she was dazzled by the fact that the brilliant American novelist was so taken by her. (I've read *Henderson's Can*, by the way. It is written by someone who has misunderstood both Joyce and Sinclair and has been buoyed by an overestimation of his own genius. He once admitted to me that the eleven pages of punctuation marks were, in fact, inspired by his cat stepping on his typewriter. He felt the cat was "teaching him the old ways." He was utterly blotto when he confessed this to me and had no recollection of the matter the next day. Even if he had, I doubt he would have cared. I don't think Roy had a high opinion of my intellect. But I digress.)

Billie grew up in a humble home in the East End. Her family were all in service. It was not a surprise to me that when she truly fell in love, it was with a handsome footman named Desmond Plott. She could relate to him. And he was a lovely man! So very funny. He regaled us with hilarious stories about the cook, Cloris Adder, who disliked his flippant attitude and was terribly unkind to him. He was sure that she'd given him a spoiled portion of food, just to make him ill. He and Billie carried on a clandestine affair whenever we visited Wuthers, and he visited her on all his days off. They became quite serious about each other, but it was all kept very quiet because of Billie's fame. She even pretended to see other men to hide her genuine love from the prying eyes of the press.

    That New Year's Eve, tensions were simmering. Felix and Desmond had both proclaimed their love for Billie, and each was aware of the other. Billie did not care for Felix, but it was exciting for her to be the center of this romantic entanglement. Desmond, however, was jealous. As a servant, he could not sit with us. He was not of our status. It was unfair and frustrating, so he drank heavily that night.

    Meanwhile, Roy was oblivious to this. He told me privately that this was the night he would tell Billie how he felt. I thought the whole thing was simply an absurd bit of fun. A comedy. I watched Billie rebuff Felix (which delighted me), and then, when Desmond vanished from the gathering, Billie said she was going to go and find him. I was distracted by my own dalliance with someone else at the party and wished her good luck.

    The next morning, I stopped by Billie's room so that we could go together to breakfast and found her awake and fretting. There had been a terrible scene the night before. She had found Desmond outside and the two were in a romantic embrace at the folly by the point when Roy Peterson appeared. Roy was enraged at seeing Billie with Desmond. The two men began to argue. Billie tried to talk Roy into going back to the house. At some point, she realized that an earring she'd been wearing had come off, and she retraced her steps trying to find it. She located it and returned a few minutes later. Both men were gone. She did not see Desmond in the dark water, and likely did not think to look there.

    She returned to the house and went to bed, only to hear of the discovery of Desmond's body in the morning. She knew Roy had to have killed him—by accident or on purpose, she did not know.

Later that day I went outside and had a look at the pond. There are several large statues that surround the pond—one is a dancing nymph with an extended foot. I found a small streak of blood on this, just a very small amount that someone had tried to wipe away.

Meanwhile, Roy had gone running to Alfred. Alfred was concerned about a dead body on his property. If the police investigated, they might discover the rooms in the basement where he has his secret ceremonies. (He is the head of something he calls the Octopus Society and it involves lots of robes and chanting and quite a lot of sex. It's all silly and harmless, but there are many important people who would not want it to be known that they spent their nights naked and in chains at Wuthers.) The whole thing had been covered up by lunch. Even the tiny spot of blood on the foot of the statue was gone.

Billie was not the same after that. She had truly loved Desmond, and she felt she had caused his death. She became more and more wild and despairing. Mabel was no help at all. She was jealous of Billie's accomplishments, and frankly seemed delighted to see her sister so miserable. Billie started using more and more drugs. Ambrose and I began to worry for her, to beg her to stop.

On the night she died, she was in strange, bright spirits. I thought she was improving. We went to the Never-Never Ball, and she danced like a woman possessed. Cocaine, of course. Too much of it. She came both to me and to Ambrose, demanding more. We flatly denied her. She then appealed to Felix, who was happy to be of service.

I do not know if the overdose she took that night was intentional or accidental. I can only tell you that I was not surprised. I had felt it coming. The horror of it all began to eat at me—two people dead, and no justice. I was despairing until I came up with what I began to call my Little Project. All that was crooked would be made straight. Ambrose and I had gotten her interested in cocaine. Felix had given her all she needed to overdose on the night of her death. Mabel did nothing but profit from her sister's death. Roy had killed Desmond and Alfred helped him get away with it. Cloris Adder had been cruel to Desmond, so her appearance in the matter was purely in tribute to him.

I created the letters, taking great care that there were no fingerprints or identifying marks, but making sure that the contents spelled out something incriminating about each person, including myself. I was creating my own dramatic court. Charges would be brought to expose us all. I chose Tootley Row as the setting for my trial. I know the house back to front. Also, I'd met a lovely man named Phillip at a party there once who whispered a little secret about a box by the kitchen window with a key inside. I had a way in.

    In murder as in comedy, timing is everything. I'd set everything to go like clockwork. The first step took place at Gibbons Restaurant, as you saw. It's nothing at all to dress as a man, especially if you are not going to be closely examined. A coat, a moustache, a hat. I was wearing a pair of Ambrose's shoes that I'd taken weeks earlier. Ambrose is always misplacing things.

    I was surprised to see Roy sitting at the window. He always sat in the back. Perhaps he had realized he was being followed. This made things easier for me. I'd worked up an elaborate sketch to talk my way to the back of the restaurant; now all I had to do was pretend to be surprised to see the famous novelist Roy Peterson sitting by the window. I went inside and asked for an autograph in a manner calculated to enrage him. He did not disappoint. He yelled at me and I fumbled with my umbrella, dropping it. I am a good comedian, Detective. I am quick. I dumped the contents of a vial of morphine into his powerful cocktail. (It is not important where I got the morphine. It was the same place Billie got hers—a quite legitimate doctor who will give anything to a woman who bats her eyelashes and has ready money.) I gave him quite a large dose. I was going to kill Roy Peterson, but I am not without mercy. He would not feel it. I needed him not to feel it to make this work. I walked out of Gibbons with my head down in what I am sure they thought was embarrassment.

    I had pre-arranged the business with the napkin, as you discovered. People who drink four or five cocktails an hour need the loo, as you noted. This was key to my plan. I had to disable the one at Gibbons. I left the note and money with someone at a nearby shop. I assure you that they are innocent of any knowledge of the murder.

    I dropped the note at the tailor's shop at 8:40. (The hair stuck to the tailor's envelope—was that a bridge too far? It was a loose one of Mabel's. I plucked it off the back of her dress at some point and kept it. "Oh, you have a hair on your back, let me get that for you." How kind of me. I had to throw suspicion in as many directions as possible, and frankly, Mabel deserved her moment under the microscope.) I then walked to Tootley Row. Time to prepare for the next act.

Ambrose, I saw, was peering out the curtain from time to time, so I had to be careful as I made my way down the steps to the kitchen entrance. If spotted, all anyone would see was a man with an umbrella. They would probably think I was George, the valet. I broke the window with a bit of brick and undid the latch. I reached inside for the key in the box and let myself in. (Naturally, I wore gloves.)

As an actress, I know how to change quickly. The man everyone saw in Gibbons wore a buttoned-up coat and carried a shopping bag. Under the coat, I wore my dress, tucked up into the waist of a pair of men's trousers. I wriggled out of the coat, trousers, and men's shoes. I ripped off the wig and moustache. It took a minute, start to finish. I put the trousers in with a pile of laundry, and placed Ambrose's shoes in George's room. George cares for all of Ambrose's clothing and polishes his shoes, so it wouldn't be so unusual to find them there. It would cause George some confusion, but that was fine.

Now it was time to do what I had come to do. I crept up the servants' stairs in my stocking feet and hung the coat on the rack. I waited there, with the door open just a crack.

I chose Mabel as the first to arrive in order to keep Ambrose busy, and to give him some protection. I didn't want him left alone with Roy, in case any questions came up about the morphine. I listened with amusement as he greeted her. I followed the time carefully, and at 9:10, Roy came to the door. The morphine would have been starting to take effect, so he would have been slurring and at least partially numb. Now I just needed him to go to the loo. Oh, how I worried! If he didn't, this would all be for nothing. My only backup was that the morphine might kill him, but that would not have been as good.

He must have fussed around at bit at first, but finally, back he came, right past the door where I was hiding. And then, as he left the toilet, I reached out and stabbed him in the left side.

I thought it would be harder, both physically and mentally. But I kept thinking about Billie and Desmond. I kept their image fixed in my mind, and then I just thrust my arm forward. It was actually quite easy. (I'd rehearsed, of course. I am a professional. I'd learned the best place to land a blow that would cause a massive bleed and practiced on various cuts of meat. I was so pleased to hear how well I'd placed it!)

Roy didn't see me, but he noticed that something had struck his side. He seemed to think he had bumped into the coatrack. Though he felt it and winced, it did not appear to cause him a tremendous amount of pain.

After Roy went back into the sitting room, I took the ice pick back downstairs and wrapped it in a bit of newspaper and put it in my purse. I cleaned a spot of blood from my hands. I put on my women's shoes, which were in the shopping bag along with my purse. I took a moment in George's room to clean my face of any spirit gum using my cold cream, then I applied some lipstick and arranged my hair.

Then, carrying the bag with the trousers, wig, mustache, gloves, and hat, I stepped outside with my umbrella. I tossed the bag onto the back platform of a passing bus. And voila! There I was, on the front step, right on time. The only thing off about my appearance was my lack of a coat, but I could put that down to being a silly person who heard that coats were out of fashion.

I had given myself the 9:40 entrance cue. When I entered the sitting room, I believe Roy was either already gone or was on the very moment of passing. I watched for any rise and fall of his chest. I never saw him take a breath. The expression on his face was peaceful.

The others were fighting about the letters, accusing one another of sending them. They fought like cats and dogs, particularly Mabel and Alfred. All except for Ambrose, who regarded it all with some amusement and detachment. I know on some level he took it to heart. He knew what we had done to Billie. I met his eye more than once, and while I do not think he ever suspected me, we had an understanding. We were guilty. I was just far guiltier because of the thing I was doing at that very moment.

Then, right on time, the constable came to the door. Mr. Finsdale's timing is as impeccable as his stitching (he resized a dress for me once). The only thing I had left to do was drop the ice pick on the floor in the confusion and toss the bit of newspaper onto the fire. I wanted the mystery to be total. How was this man stabbed in front of everyone? It would be in all the papers. The letters would get out. Billie and Desmond would get the justice they deserved.

    I knew things would happen along the way that I would not be able to account for, but I assumed they might help by causing confusion. I was telling the truth when I said the cocaine found in the chair I was sitting in was not mine, and that I had stopped taking it after Billie died. From the look of the container, I believe it belongs to Alfred. He loves the stuff. Alfred also panicked and burned his letter. Alfred likes to cover things up.

    The note that said I SAW WOT YOU DONE in Roy's pocket took me entirely off guard when I heard of it. I suspect someone shoved it under his door at Wuthers and he had kept it, terrified, wondering where it had come from. I think some of the servants had a good idea of what had happened, and that note was one of them speaking up. I hope it tormented him.

    Ambrose is a very smart man. He'd been thinking through the events and had just spoken to George, his valet, who had just come back from an interview with the police. Ambrose found out about the spare key. He questioned George more carefully and found out that his missing shoes had turned up downstairs. Ambrose knew about Desmond and Billie, he knew how I felt after Billie died. He'd also found out that George gave the police a photograph taken hours before the murder.

Ambrose had to be interviewed again the next day so the police could find out what he knew about the spare key. He tried to throw suspicion in other directions, and once again made me out to be a bit simple. He asked to see the photograph. Once he saw the spare coat, he knew. Shoes. A suddenly appearing coat on the rack in the hall. Someone had come in through the basement in a disguise. Someone had been in the hall. Only I came without a coat, and I came after Roy had been stabbed.

That night, he came to visit me and advised me to leave the country, go to Paris for a while, or America, but I refused. I think you understand why. I had to watch all the secrets come out. I had to know that Desmond's death was brought into the open and Billie's story told.

I do not want to be hanged, detective, but I have always accepted that I must pay for my crime. I have a full package of Slumberaid and another vial of morphine. Final justice will be served and Billie and I will be together again.

I have enclosed a photograph I took of Desmond and Billie at their happiest. This is how they should be remembered.

Thank you for appreciating this, my greatest performance.

xoxo,
Vita

1 3 5 7 9 10 8 6 4 2

Harvill, an imprint of Vintage, is part of the Penguin Random House group of companies

Vintage, Penguin Random House UK, One Embassy Gardens,
8 Viaduct Gardens, London SW11 7BW

penguin.co.uk/vintage
global.penguinrandomhouse.com

First published in Great Britain by Harvill in 2025
First published in the United States of America by Ten Speed Press in 2025

Copyright © Maureen Johnson and Jay Cooper 2025

The moral right of the authors has been asserted

Textural background elements courtesy of Adobe Stock

Penguin Random House values and supports copyright. Copyright fuels creativity, encourages diverse voices, promotes freedom of expression and supports a vibrant culture. Thank you for purchasing an authorised edition of this book and for respecting intellectual property laws by not reproducing, scanning or distributing any part of it by any means without permission. You are supporting authors and enabling Penguin Random House to continue to publish books for everyone. No part of this book may be used or reproduced in any manner for the purpose of training artificial intelligence technologies or systems. In accordance with Article 4(3) of the DSM Directive 2019/790, Penguin Random House expressly reserves this work from the text and data mining exception.

Printed and bound in Great Britain by Clays Ltd, Elcograf S.p.A.

The authorised representative in the EEA is Penguin Random House Ireland,
Morrison Chambers, 32 Nassau Street, Dublin D02 YH68

A CIP catalogue record for this book is available from the British Library

ISBN 9781787305533

Penguin Random House is committed to a sustainable future
for our business, our readers and our planet. This book is made
from Forest Stewardship Council® certified paper.

MAUREEN JOHNSON and JAY COOPER are the bestselling duo behind *Your Guide to Not Getting Murdered in a Quaint English Village*. Johnson is also the #1 *New York Times*-bestselling author of young adult novels, including the Shades of London series and the Stevie Bell mysteries. Cooper has written and/or illustrated more than twenty-five books for kids, including *The Spy Next Door*, and designs advertising campaigns for Broadway shows.